AT DUSK

HWANG SOK-YONG was born in 1943 and is arguably Korea's most renowned author. In 1993, he was sentenced to seven years in prison for an unauthorised trip to the North to promote exchange between artists in the two Koreas. Five years later, he was released on a special pardon by the new president. The recipient of Korea's highest literary prizes, he has been shortlisted for the Prix Femina Etranger and was awarded the Emile Guimet Prize for Asian Literature for *At Dusk*. His novels and short stories are published in North and South Korea, Japan, China, France, Germany, and the United States. Previous novels include *The Ancient Garden*, *The Story of Mister Han*, *The Guest*, and *The Shadow of Arms*.

SORA KIM-RUSSELL is a literary translator based in Seoul. She primarily translates works by Hwang Sok-yong, Pyun Hye-young, and Kim Un-su. Her full list of publications can be found at www.sorakimrussell.com.

AT DUSK

Hwang Sok-yong

Translated by Sora Kim-Russell

SCRIBE
Melbourne • London

Scribe Publications
2 John St, Clerkenwell, London, WC1N 2ES, United Kingdom
18–20 Edward St, Brunswick, Victoria 3056, Australia
3754 Pleasant Ave, Suite 100, Minneapolis, Minnesota 55409 USA

First published in Korean as *Haejil Muryeop* by Munhakdongne 2018

English translation first published in Australia, New Zealand, and the
United Kingdom by Scribe 2018
Published in the United States by Scribe 2019
Reprinted 2021

Typeset in 11.65/17.15 pt Adobe Garamond by J&M Typesetting P/L
Printed and bound in United States of America by Ingram Content Group

Scribe Publications is committed to the sustainable use of natural resources
and the use of paper products made responsibly from those resources.

This book is published with the support of the
Literature Translation Institute of Korea (LTI Korea)

LTI Korea
Literature Translation Institute of Korea

9781947534667 (US edition)
9781911617235 (UK edition)
9781925322934 (Australian edition)
9781925693140 (ebook)

Catalogue records for this book are available from the National Library of Australia
and the British Library.

scribepublications.com
scribepublications.co.uk
scribepublications.com.au

1

My lecture ended.

The projector clicked off and the screen went dark.

I drank half of the water that had been placed on the podium for me and stepped down from the stage to join the audience members, who'd risen from their seats and were already chatting amongst themselves. The lecture had been on 'Urban Design and the Development of Old City Centres', and given the decent turnout, I assumed they all had a vested interest in the subject. The section chief for the private sector planning commission at City Hall guided me into the lobby outside the lecture hall. Everyone was streaming towards the entrance. A young woman swam against the crowd of people and approached me.

Do you have a moment? she asked.

She was dressed casually in jeans and a T-shirt, no make-up, hair in a simple bob cut. I stopped and looked at her.

I have something for you, she said.

Puzzled, I looked down at the piece of paper she was holding out. A name was printed on it in large letters, along with what looked like a phone number in much smaller print.

What is this? I asked, but she was already backing away hesitantly.

Someone you used to know … She asks that you please call her.

She vanished into the crowd before I could ask anything else.

Not long after, a text message from Yoon Byeonggu's wife had me heading out of the city back to the small town of Yeongsan. Byeonggu was an old childhood friend. We'd gone to primary school together in Yeongsan, and had grown up next door to each other. Most of the people who lived there back then either owned small shops along the newly paved main road or held government jobs working for the county office, the school, or the township office. As for those who lived in the nice, traditional Korean-style houses with big courtyards, they owned all of the farmland in the county. My father supported our family on the tiny wages he made as a clerk in the township office.

Despite the ravages of the Korean War, Yeongsan's location, tucked inside the Nakdong River beachhead, had kept it safe and unchanged. My mother had told me that my father was able to land his position at the township office by virtue of having gone to war and received a medal for his distinguished service in some Battle of Something-or-other Hill, on top of which, even before all of that, he'd worked as an errand boy for the county office during Japanese rule. In a town full of country bumpkins, my father had a primary school education and could read and write in both Japanese and Chinese. Lined up evenly along his desk were old books, yellowed and dog-eared, with titles like *Compendium of the Six Major Laws* and *The Science of Public Administration*. I'm sure it was thanks to those books that he was later able to leave the countryside for the big city and find work as a clerk in a notary office. Though we were poor, we had his monthly civil servant's salary and the annual share of the harvest from my mother's family land. She had inherited some paddies — enough to plant about five bushels of rice seeds every year — from her father when she married.

The house we lived in was in the foothills of the mountain that rose up from the edge of town. It was a traditional ilja-style home: long and straight like the numeral 1, with three rooms side-by-side and a daecheong maru, a wooden-floored breezeway, right in the middle. Byeonggu's house was just up the slope from ours. It was two rooms and a kitchen — a hut, really — made from clay walls and a thatched roof that was later changed to slate.

Though Byeonggu and I were old friends, the truth was that I hardly knew him. Around the time I finished primary school, my family left Yeongsan and moved to Seoul. I didn't see Byeonggu again until years later, when we were nearing forty. I bumped into him one day in a hotel coffeeshop somewhere in downtown Seoul.

Remember me?

At first, when I heard his thick Gyeongsang Province accent, I had no idea who he was. He was dressed in a navy suit with his shirt collar on the outside, in the style of high-ranking government employees at the time. To my surprise, the moment he said the names Yoon Byeonggu and Yeongsan, the nickname that I'd long forgotten came floating out of my mouth as if by magic.

Tan Goguma. You're Burnt Sweet Potato, aren't you?

It's hard to know what to say to someone you haven't seen in over twenty years. It's the same even if they're a blood relative. For the most part, you ask how they've been and inquire after each other's families, then grab a cup of coffee together, maybe exchange business cards or contact information, and make vague promises to get together sometime for a drink. After which you might ring each other up just once or twice, or more likely never see them again at all, and on the rare occasion that you do end up meeting for a drink, the evening proves so dull that you don't stay for a second round. Everyone is busy tending to their own interests, and unless those interests are shared by your own kin, then no matter how closely related you are, you'll still never see them outside of family reunions.

What brought Byeonggu and I back together was that I was at Hyeonsan Architecture, and he had just taken over Yeongnam Construction, one of the main construction outfits at the time. The moment he heard me say his old nickname, Tan Goguma, tears welled up in his eyes, and he grabbed my hand and stammered out his astonishment at the fact that I hadn't forgotten it.

His childhood home had stood on the other side of a stone wall from ours, close to the large zelkova tree that grew on the left side of our yard. Every morning, he would stick his head over the wall and holler for me to walk to school with him. His was the last house in the neighbourhood; everything beyond was public land, starting from the grove of young pines that grew on the lower slope of the mountain. After the war, former tenant farmers from nearby had slowly gathered in the area to build shacks, nabbing bits of land for themselves and building rough walls from mud and stone, until a dozen families were living there. They eked out a living by doing odd jobs in town, working as plasterers or carpenters, or carrying out chores at the district office, while helping out the local farmers every harvest in exchange for food. I was born in one of those houses, and though I don't remember for sure, I think Byeonggu's family moved next door to us when he was in the third grade. He said hello to me first the day they moved in, and we spent that same afternoon playing on the mountain behind our houses. I could still remember Byeonggu's mother, a very kind woman, bringing us a basket of sweet potatoes that she'd harvested at the farm where she worked, telling us to give them a taste. He often brought a couple of sweet potatoes to school for his lunch. His father would disappear for days at a time, only to return home drunk and shouting his head off at his family or taking a swing at his wife. They said he worked as a foreman on a construction site in a nearby city.

I'd never forgotten about Byeonggu, all because of the time we'd gone up in the mountain behind our houses to roast sweet potatoes over a campfire, and accidentally set off a wildfire instead. While we were distracted with peeling hot sweet potatoes, embers had blown into the dried grass. We ran around in a panic, trying to stamp out the flames, pulling off our shirts to smother them, but the fire spread before we could even blink. As a last resort, I'd raced downhill, shouting, Fire! Fire! The grown-ups came running out of the houses. Everyone in the neighbourhood flocked up the mountain, and after a great deal of commotion that lasted until well past sundown, they finally managed to put out the flames.

Meanwhile, Byeonggu and I hid in the community centre across from the district office. The centre had been used as a Shinto shrine during Japanese rule, but when we lived there, it was used as an assembly hall-slash-taekwondo studio. We fell asleep leaning against each other in the darkened centre. Our families and neighbours were stuck searching for us in the mountains until late into the night. The next morning, we woke and went to school only to find out how famous we'd become. We were punished by being made to stand in the teachers' office, holding signs that read, BEWARE OF FIRE. That must have been when Byeonggu got the nickname Tan Goguma, or Burnt Sweet Potato, but I can't remember who was the first to call him that. With his short, stocky body and eyes that sparkled with cleverness in his round, dark face, it was a fitting nickname.

It was mere coincidence that I had studied architecture and made a career of it and that Byeonggu had come to own a construction company, but after meeting again in our forties, we were like hand in glove. Because we needed each other.

Of course, we all like to think that our own stories of difficult childhoods and overcoming adversity are the stuff of tragic epics, but they're never really worth bragging about. Talking about it is as pointless as telling youngsters that they've never known true hunger, that they don't know what it was like to be the hungry kid with no lunch, trying to fill his empty stomach at the school drinking fountain.

I met Byeonggu for dinner at a Japanese restaurant, where he filled me in on everything that had happened to him after my family left Yeongsan. Byeonggu's grades had been terrible, and his parents couldn't afford the monthly school fees anyway, so he'd dropped out sometime in the fifth grade. He loafed about for a while before becoming a newspaper delivery boy, then worked as a hawker at a bus terminal, and finally, in his early teens, became an assistant truck driver. His father left for the big city and never returned, his kindhearted mother found work in a restaurant in town, and his little sister ran away from home to attend beauty school. Byeonggu and I both did our army service in the mid-70s. I finished a little later than him since I completed my service after spending a few years in college. He was deployed to an engineering battalion and received heavy-equipment training, which proved pivotal to his career path. Immediately after leaving the army, he got his heavy-equipment certification and leapt with both feet into the rural modernisation project that was in full swing at the time.

The first thing he did was rent an excavator and join the farmland improvement effort. This was the time of the New Village Movement, when land abandoned by former tenant farmers and small farmers who didn't own enough land to subsist on was incorporated and restructured into mid-sized farm villages. Farmland was resectioned and waterways were redug. The project was undertaken by country offices along with powerful community leaders in each area, and working below them was Byeonggu, who fancied himself their hands and feet. For the first several years, all he did was increase his heavy machinery by a few pieces, but after winning a project to build arterial roads through the countryside, he left the township and began working at the provincial level. His circle of acquaintances widened to include national assemblymen and judges and prosecutors. He had a selection of business cards, each stamped with his many job titles: Construction Company Owner, Political Party Consultant, Juvenile Guidance Commissioner, Scholarship Committee Director, Junior Chamber Member, Rotary Club Member, Lions Club Member, and so on, and so on. When I met him again, he'd taken over a bankrupt construction company and had begun building apartment complexes in the major cities. We had immediately started calling each other up all the time and even went in on a few prospective business projects together.

His wife's text message read: 'He collapsed. He'd been looking for you for a while, since before he got sick. Please come visit.'

What made me agree to go back to Yeongsan? I really didn't want to. Maybe it was because of what Kim Kiyoung had said to me a few days earlier: 'You say buildings are made of space, time, and humanity? Is there really any humanity in architecture? If there were, you'd have to regret what you did. You and the others at Hyeonsan need to think on your sins.'

Kiyoung had graduated ahead of me from the same college. I just smiled and avoided arguing with him, but not because he was in the final stages of cancer. I liked the guy. I liked his foolish naivety, his unrequited love of the world and people. I didn't give him shit for it. Others liked to say that he called himself an idealist because he had no talent, but I felt that *was* his talent. The magnanimity I felt towards him probably came from the fact that I'd long ago resolved not to care too much about a world that didn't care about me in return, and had therefore distanced myself from him as well. Back then, I'd decided that I could not trust the world or other people. After a while, being ambitious means having to sift out the few values we feel like keeping and toss the rest, or twist them to suit ourselves. Even the tiny handful of values that remain just get stuffed into the attic of memory, like some old thing bought and used up long ago. What are buildings made of? In the end, money and power. They alone decide which memories will take shape and survive.

Yeongsan lay just over the mountain pass. I thought about the night my family left the countryside to move to Seoul. My parents rode in the cab of the moving truck next to the driver, while my little brother and I squatted in the back between the boxes. A basin filled with miscellaneous kitchen utensils shook and let out a terrible racket with each bounce and rattle of the truck on the dirt road. Unsurprisingly, more than half of our dishes ended up broken. We drove until daybreak, only stopping to stretch our legs and get something to eat when we reached the highway that led north to Seoul. We hadn't eaten dinner before leaving town, so we wolfed down bowls of steaming-hot rice soup. My mother muttered something about penniless people fleeing under cover of night, and burst into tears.

I returned to Yeongsan only once after that, about fifteen years ago. At the time, Byeonggu was looking to buy a house in our old hometown, and had been going back and forth between there and Seoul. He said to me in this very grave voice, No one should ever forget their roots. I felt embarrassed when he said that. He ended up buying a pine-covered hill overlooking the reservoir, thus breaking up the ancestral home of the big landowning Cho family. There was already little left of the original village by then. Everyone says that things move slower in the countryside, but to those who have left it for the city, the countryside changes like a film on fast forward. While you're busy debating whether or not to go back home for a visit, wondering if there is some compelling enough reason to go, ten years seem to flash by in a single day, the familiar faces all vanish, and the same buildings and scenery that you see in Seoul now occupy both sides of your town's once quaint main street. Then that too passes away as quickly as a landscape seen through the window of a speeding car.

The moment she saw me, Byeonggu's wife started dabbing at her eyes with a handkerchief. She'd started out as an elementary school teacher but married Byeonggu in the early 1980s, right at the peak of his career. I remember thinking that even his wedding had been a practical affair and not too showy. His wife stepped out of his hospital room and muttered something, almost under her breath, the moment we were face to face.

I told him to stay out of politics …

He'd come out of surgery in a coma. It might have been a blessing in disguise. He was due to appear before the prosecutor in a week. Most likely, whoever else was involved would thank their lucky stars when they heard the news. I sat at his bedside while he lay there as if dead, surrounded by all sorts of medical equipment. The oxygen mask covered half of his face. His wife told me that their eldest son had suggested moving him to a bigger, provincial hospital, but they were worried that his condition might worsen en route. Over dinner, I asked their son why they'd called me. Their son explained that Byeonggu had been talking about wanting to build a memorial hall on the spot where his childhood home had stood.

Dad said that his house and your house were on about five hundred pyeong of land. He wants you to draw up the blueprint so they can put up a building and start a cultural foundation.

I started to laugh but managed to keep my voice even.

You should hold that thought until your father is back on his feet.

I could tell that Byeonggu's son, who managed his

father's business in Seoul, knew as well as I did that it wasn't the right time to have that discussion. He kept looking at his phone during dinner and stepped outside at one point with it to raise his voice and shout orders at someone. He said that he was concerned because country towns like Yeongsan were losing people. A lot of places were on their way to becoming ghost towns, places where the majority of the houses either sat empty or were occupied by a single elderly person. He acted like he knew all about life in the countryside, and kept remarking that it'd been that way for a long time now, as if all the young people had just dried up and blown away. The fact of the matter was that he and I were both the type who found ourselves debating once or twice a year at most whether to make a hometown visit, so he wasn't exactly wrong.

It was already dark, so I headed for the motel where Byeonggu's son had reserved a room for me. The motel had all sorts of modern equipment. Security cameras were installed at each end of the hallway, and everything in the room, from the lamps to the TV set, was controlled by a single remote. It was hard to fall asleep in a new place. I fussed with the curtains, trying to block out the light that seeped through, while grumbling about why such a tiny backwater town needed so many streetlights.

I woke early. The glowing clock face told me it was 7:10 a.m. I'd been a late sleeper ever since my younger years. That was partly the fault of my line of work: unlike most businesses, working in an architecture firm meant that I only had to worry about my own part of the project, and that I didn't have to trouble myself with the miscellany since I was there to be 'creative'. While running my own firm, I only had to go into the office a couple of times a week, and even then I would roll in sometime after ten and leave early if there wasn't much to do. Having always worked as a night owl, I'd long been in the habit of waking and starting my own day long after everyone else had already clocked in at their jobs.

Though it was still early, I couldn't just lie there. The road outside the motel took me straight to the bus terminal. Country folk are a hard-working lot. The front of the station was already bustling with people and taxis. This time, as I walked along the main street, I found myself grumbling about why such a small town had so many cars. The low-roofed shops from the old days were all gone; each side of the street was lined with two- and three-storey buildings, and the street itself had been significantly widened. Only the layout of the town remained the same.

I took a right at the intersection and went down the street next to the county office and past the community centre. When the road led uphill, I paused to look left and right but didn't see the pine grove that should have been there. The old alleyway was gone, replaced by a paved, two-lane road. Gone, too, were the stone walls that had once lined both sides of the alley. Instead, more rows of perfectly square two- and three-storey buildings led all the way down. I eyeballed the shape of the mountaintop and walked uphill to the left. When I spotted the cement sewer cover, I knew I was going the right way. A small stream used to flow there. My father had fallen in once while walking home drunk, and I'd caught frogs in it.

I saw a couple of houses between the fields, but I did not see our house. When I'd come fifteen years ago, someone had been living in it despite its dilapidated state; later, it looked abandoned, until finally it was demolished. I still remembered the large tree that had stood in the corner of the yard, overlooking Byeonggu's house. The tree was gone. Or rather, its stump was still there, but the rest had been chopped down. Mushrooms of all sizes were sprouting from it. A large pepper field, the ridges lined with black vinyl sheeting, stretched from there to where Byeonggu's house had stood. The trees that blanketed the mountainside looked denser and a darker green than before.

I couldn't wrap my brain around how civilised it had become — my hometown, which now had more people who'd left than people who'd stayed. The boxy two- and three-storey cement buildings that occupied downtown from the shopping area all the way to the residential area looked bleaker than ever. There was no smoke from cooking fires curling up from low roofs. Looking down on it from the hillside, it could've been any other small city, or worse, the outskirts of Seoul. It was as if me and Tan Goguma, my long-departed parents, and even my hometown itself had never really existed.

That weekend, I got a long-distance call from my daughter, who coolly recounted everything that had happened in my absence over the past month. She was my only child, and now she was living in the United States. She had graduated from medical school, become a doctor at a major hospital, and married a professor. She'd gone abroad for her education and ended up marrying an American citizen and, of course, becoming an American citizen herself. After our daughter settled down, my wife travelled back and forth between both countries, but now she too seemed intent on staying there. It had been several years since she'd last come home. Nearly all of my wife's relatives were living in the US by that point, and our own marriage had been showing signs of strain for the past decade or so and was now so out of joint that there was little chance of putting it all straight again. My daughter told me about my wife's new apartment. She described the housewarming, all the aunts and other relatives who'd come. How's your health? she asked. Mum said don't forget to take your blood pressure pills. It was clear my wife had no intention of coming back to me, seeing as how she'd just moved into an apartment close to where our daughter lived.

For the first time in a long time, I found myself craving

a cigarette and searched all over for one. There had to be a pack of Marlboro Reds somewhere. I always reached for one when I got stuck while sketching out an idea. I found my lighter next to the desk lamp and rummaged through the desk drawers, then started checking the pockets of all my suits hanging in the closet. Finally, my fingers traced the outline of a pack. As I fumbled for it, something fell onto the floor. Two business cards and a folded-up note. One of the cards was for a city hall employee, the other was for some magazine reporter, and the note ... I set it on top of my desk and lit a cigarette. I stared at the name printed in large letters above the phone number, repeating the syllables over and over in my head. Cha Soona. A name from decades past that I'd long since forgotten. I pictured how the young woman at the lecture hall last week had handed the note to me. I'd had an appointment to give an interview for some architecture magazine immediately after the lecture, and then I'd gone drinking with a group of people. After that, things had been so hectic that I'd forgotten all about the note.

After a great deal of hesitation, I pulled the phone on the desk towards me and dialled the number. It rang for a long time before going to voicemail. I debated what to say but then hung up and sent a text message over my cell phone instead.

This is Park Minwoo. Please give me a call when you can.

17

When I got to the office, Song, a fellow architect, said, Are you going to the thing for Kim Kiyoung today?

What thing?

His doctor said he doesn't have much time left, Song explained, so a few of us decided to take him on a day trip, to get him some fresh air, change of scenery.

In that case, sure. Where are you taking him?

Out to Ganghwa Island.

I decided to ride with Song instead of taking the chauffeured company car.

As we drove along Olympic Highway, Song said, I heard President Im of Daedong Construction has been named.

It was easy enough to guess what rumours he'd heard, but I pretended I knew nothing.

Named? What're you talking about?

They say there's bad blood between him and the current administration.

Daedong Construction had hired us for the Hangang Digital Centre project. More than half of the skyscraper was already built. I deliberately kept my voice neutral.

We don't need to worry about that. All we have to do is finish the job we were given.

We still need to watch our backs.

It sounded like he'd been reading the papers. The story going around was that the construction company was under secret investigation and that the Asia World project Daedong was promoting in the suburbs had hit some funding problems and was on the verge of running aground.

I kept my voice cheerful as I said, Been a long time since I've taken an outing like this. I hope you're not trying to spoil the fun.

Song changed the subject.

This trip won't cure Kiyoung's cancer but it should lift his spirits.

It definitely will. He's always been an optimist.

There was no traffic since it was a weekday, so we made quick time along Olympic Highway and soon were crossing Choji Bridge onto Ganghwa Island. We parked in a lot near an intersection and went into a coffee shop. Lee Youngbin, who was now a professor, had arrived first and waved us over. He was the same age as me. Though we'd graduated from different schools, we'd gotten to know each other from competing in the same design contests, always jockeying for number one, and had grown our businesses at the same time as well. We'd competed for some projects, collaborated on others. Like Kiyoung, he'd gotten his architecture degree in Europe. Our firm's work was much better than his, but he was a native Seoulite from a wealthy family. He'd retired early and gone into teaching, and was now a so-called critic, in name only. He was dressed casually and wearing a baseball cap. He seemed surprised to see me.

You came all the way here? You're usually so busy.

I haven't seen Kiyoung in a long time.

A van pulled into the parking lot, and a familiar-looking younger man came running into the coffeeshop. It was the editor from the architecture magazine. He looked around and then came over to us.

We made a reservation near Dongmak Beach. Let's go.

Kiyoung waved from the front passenger seat when he saw us coming. We formed a caravan of three vehicles. It was early in the season, and the beach was quiet except for a handful of families and couples on outings. We sat at a table in a restaurant overlooking the water. Kiyoung had lost a lot of weight since I'd last seen him a few months ago, and he was hiding the hair loss from the chemo under an old fedora. There were around ten of us altogether, including two journalists from the magazine, a gallery curator, Kiyoung's wife, and his architecture interns. Kiyoung and his wife, and Youngbin and I sat apart from the others. We ordered grilled clams and sushi — all small fish, like pomfret and herring.

We brought up the idea of hiking Manisan, which was something we'd done together often back in the early days of Hyeonsan Architecture. Back then, we were all young and had just returned from studying abroad in foreign countries, which had made us fearless. Though our definitions of success varied, Kiyoung still ran the same small atelier as he did back then; Youngbin, having never managed to create anything memorable, had retreated into academia and was all talk and no action; while I had once run an entrepreneurial architecture firm that had employed close to a hundred people. I guess we'd all run out of steam as we got older. Luckily, the financial crisis came along, and I had to trim the fat, converting to a more streamlined business with twenty employees.

Kiyoung seemed to be in an especially good mood; it'd been a long time since he'd gotten out of the city. Each time he smiled, his face, which had shrunken from illness, crumpled into wrinkles. Despite his doctor's advice to eat a lot of high-protein food in order to overcome the effects of the cancer treatment, he ate only a few bites of the abalone and clams that his wife gave him.

Let's be honest, Kiyoung said. We know I don't have long to live. Have any of you been to England and ridden the London Eye? Youngbin said that he had, and Kiyoung nodded. They say it takes an hour for the wheel to make one full revolution. You know what the Buddha said. The wheel of life takes a hundred years to turn. Which means that none of us make it all the way around before we have to get off.

After a hundred years, most of the people here would be gone. The world would be full of new people. Everyone thinks it's good to be an architect, because your buildings will stand long after you're gone, but for all you know, they could be left looking greedy and ugly. After lunch, the younger folk went for a walk on the beach, strolling along and tossing shrimp chips to the seagulls. We didn't make it to the Hwado Township side of Manisan until close to dusk. We parked and got out. The sun was setting. It was slipping very slowly, one inch at a time, below the horizon.

Youngbin mentioned Byeonggu.

Isn't President Yoon of Yeongnam Construction an old childhood friend of yours? I met him a few times through you, back in the Hyeonsan days.

Kiyoung seemed to remember him, too. That was back when you all struck it rich, he said. Wasn't he elected to the National Assembly a couple of times?

I heard they're in trouble now over slush funds? Yoon, and now Daedong Construction? Youngbin asked, looking pointedly at me.

Just drop it.

All we did was draw up some designs for them. I heard Yoon had a stroke and is in a coma.

I told them about my trip to Yeongsan. About how the houses and stone walls and paths were all gone, and how even the site where my childhood home had stood was now bare save for a tree stump.

Everyone's hometown is disappearing, I said.

Kiyoung gazed out at where the sky met the water before turning to look at us.

And you're the jerks who tore it all down. Ah, look at that beautiful sunset!

On our way back to downtown Seoul, everyone parted

ways. Youngbin came with me to my office. We hadn't planned it in advance, but the two of us decided to swing by a nearby wine bar. Over dinner, he suggested the idea of one last event for Kiyoung. A retrospective featuring sketches, scale models, photographs, blueprints, and other materials from Kiyoung's career. He said he'd already started raising funds for it and urged me to help out as well. I said I would.

After we were both starting to get a little drunk, Youngbin went to the restroom. When he came back, he said, completely out of the blue, Maybe it's because of spending time today with someone who's dying, but … I couldn't help thinking about those acacia trees.

Acacias?

I had no idea what he was talking about.

You remember, that redevelopment project north of the river.

As soon as he said it, I pictured those low hills, the slums that had once covered the slopes, the crowded rows of jerry-built shanties.

What about it? I muttered.

Nothing. Just thinking of old times. We bulldozed all of it.

I sat there, not saying anything for a moment, before remarking flatly, Didn't you know? I grew up in a slum, too.

Youngbin was just as unmoved.

You mentioned that to me before, he said. I know I say

this all the time, but you're one of the strong ones.

We didn't part ways until close to midnight. When I got home, I changed clothes and took out my cell phone. There were several new text messages, including one from Cha Soona.

> This is Soona. Guess I missed your call. Thank you
> for remembering me. I can't answer my phone during
> the day, but evenings are okay, even if it's late.

I hesitated for a moment, then dialled her number. It was late, but she'd sent that text barely an hour ago. I figured if she was sleeping, she would just not pick up or would have her cell turned off. I heard a faint ringtone, then a voice saying, Hello?

Hello, uh, this is Park Minwoo.

Oh, Minwoo! Do you remember me? From the noodle house … where we grew up.

Her voice hadn't changed much, despite getting older. My own voice perked up, too, as I asked where was she living now, what was she doing, how were her parents. She told me she had a business in Bucheon, that it was enough to get by on, that she'd heard about my lecture in passing, and demurred when I asked in return why she hadn't come to it herself. I told her I would have been happy to see her. She said she was old and fat now, and too shy about that to come see me. I said that we should stay in touch now that we had each other's phone numbers, or better yet, meet in person. Then we hung up.

The next day, I woke up thirsty, my head pounding. The inside of my head felt like a blank sheet of paper. But then, one by one, the sunset I'd seen from the top of a hill, the sanguine laughter of a man in the final stages of cancer, and the sound of Soona's voice over the telephone spread like ink blotches across that white paper. They felt like the tangled ends of a dream that continues upon waking, and I shook my head hard and thought, Come on already. I got some water from the fridge and swallowed two glasses in a row, then sat at the table, my mind a blank. The doorbell rang. The cleaning lady was coming today. Though I didn't feel up to it, I would have to go out.

2

Like a rusted locomotive collapsed among unmoving ruins in a field covered in weeds and wildflowers, his burial was not yet over.

The last line of the script signals the end of another long rehearsal. Tomorrow is the dress rehearsal, and the day after is opening night. The actors all scatter, while I plod upstairs to the office next to the entrance of the small theatre. My boss is on the phone but waves me in when he sees me. He takes his time finishing the call, and then checks his text messages before even speaking to me.

We got two interview requests for tomorrow, he says. Seeing as you're the director, Jung Hyung, you should be the one to give the interviews.

He says that like I'm supposed to be happy to hear it, but I am too exhausted to even respond. And I'm sick of him calling me Hyung all the time, a term of respect normally reserved for men, when I have a perfectly good name of my own: Jung Woohee. He tries to make us sound like equals when really he treats me like a slave.

I haven't eaten anything since lunch, but it's already past nine o'clock and my stomach has long since stopped growling. The work we are staging this time was adapted from a novel, the rights for which we got directly from the author. And while I understood that this meant the company didn't have to pay anyone for an original script, they still should have paid me for the work I did adapting the novel to the stage. I agreed to direct and then spent several months sweating over the script. And yet I would not even be paid a directing fee, let alone a script-writing fee. Of course, none of the actors would get paid either. But I guess we knew what we were getting into.

My boss started out as a director. I'd gone to the same school as he did. He graduated before me and put together a theatre group with me and some other classmates. After narrowly managing to squeeze some money out of his parents, who'd long since given up on him, and overcoming all of the other obstacles, he succeeded in opening a tiny basement theatre. But there are so many tiny theatres and look-alike theatre companies crammed along the street that audiences are stretched thin, and the rent just keeps getting higher by the day. Every time we open a new play, we have a full house for only the first day or two, and then the numbers quickly dwindle until, by the fifth day, we are lucky to fill even ten seats. After that, we play to an empty house. Though we get some funding from the Ministry of Culture, for the most part our expenses are covered by the venue rental fees, which really only benefit the landlord. Every week we make lists of potential supporters from anywhere we can think of and send out emails pleading for them to become regular members.

I know my boss expects me to be excited about the interviews, but I respond flatly.

Can I get an advance?

What?! An advance? He looks up at me in shock and laughs. What do you think this is? A regular workplace? You know we won't know until after opening night whether we'll have any money coming in. How much do you need anyway?

About 500,000 won.

I am thinking to myself that I need to pay off at least some of my back rent if I am to make it through the month. He takes out his wallet and opens it.

There's a little bit left from the production funds ... but you know we have to pinch every penny. I can give you 300,000.

I snatch the six 50,000-won bills from his reluctantly outstretched hand before he can change his mind. As I turn and walk out the door, he shouts.

Be here by one o'clock tomorrow! You have to give those interviews!

The rehearsal isn't until seven. Dinner will be included.

I tell him, Then call the reporters back and have them come for the rehearsal.

It is my third time directing. I came close to quitting the last time.

My name is Jung Woohee, and I'm already twenty-nine years old. I went to art school and am now a beginner playwright and director. At one point I quit theatre entirely and got a regular job in order to make ends meet. I sent my resumé to a dozen places and failed interview after interview before finally managing to land a job at a tiny publishing house. I lasted about two years. All the big, hotshot publishing houses churn out bestsellers, put up new buildings, and shower their employees with bonuses, but the lousy publishing house where I worked seemed to have no capital at all, because they never once acquired a popular translation. Instead, they stuck to dusty old classics that they didn't have to worry about paying royalties for, or else pieced together a few questionable essays and slapped a plausible-sounding title on the collection.

I did everything from editing — including rewriting, embellishing, and proofreading texts — to marketing and dealing with the authors. The only employees besides me were the boss, one of his younger colleagues, and a girl, still wet behind the ears, who'd just finished junior college. We were constantly understaffed but so eager not to miss a deadline that we never hesitated to stay late. Of course, there was no such thing as overtime pay, and I had to sate my hunger with meagre midnight snacks so as not to mess up the cozy family atmosphere we had going. I put up with it for two years because I had no better options. After paying rent and utilities, I only had enough left each month to feed myself, but just barely. And since I was like a pendulum, swinging back and forth, back and forth, between work and home, I had no time to spend money on anything else anyway. I took frequent breaks in the stairwell, driven away from my desk by the emptiness of knowing that I was wasting my youth staring at a computer monitor until my eyes were practically falling out of my head just to fix other people's writing and make their work look better. On the landing, I would squat on my heels and smoke two cigarettes in a row until my insides felt like they'd calmed down a little.

One day, I was in Daehangno, the theatre district, to meet a writer, when I bumped into one of my old theatre buddies at a cafe. He said that, as luck would have it, he'd been trying to track me down, and he asked if I could write a play for him. I'd been looking for a good excuse to quit the publishing world, so I ended up throwing myself back into the quagmire of theatre. I'd already tried clawing my way up from the bottom right after graduating university, first as a lowly staff member for a theatre company, then as an extra, but with my prospects not looking all that great, I'd decided to stop. Nevertheless, I came back, dusted off a half-finished script that I'd given up on before, and just managed to spruce it up by the deadline. That fall, I entered it into a drama festival and surprised myself by winning the New Playwright Award. All of which meant that I'd come too far to quit now. No matter what happened, I would have to find my footing on the cramped stage of this tiny theatre.

I have a widowed mother and an older sister. When I was still in college, my dad, who worked as a teacher, passed away. My sister had already finished college by then, and I managed to squeak through my remaining semesters with financial help from an uncle. And actually, even before then, I'd been attending school solely due to my mother's support: my father had stubbornly opposed my decision to major in theatre at an art college and had threatened to withhold tuition unless I chose a different major or a regional school closer to home. Even my uncle had only agreed to help pay for my last two semesters after I swore to him that I would look for a job after graduation and not pursue acting. So I realised early on that I would never get to do what I wanted as long as I was dependent on someone. My sister, as well, wasted years of her life trying to pass the teacher certification exam, and all she has to show for it is a teaching position at a middle school way out in the sticks, while our mother, who held all kinds of side jobs, including cleaning other people's houses, now gets to live a quiet life in that small town right along with my sister. I avoid calling them no matter how tough things get for me, because that is the best way I have of helping them to maintain their peaceful lives.

Two 5,000-won t-shirts and a pair of 10,000-won blue jeans are enough to get me from spring to autumn, and other than food and transportation, I don't really have any expenses. Housing costs are the biggest challenge when it comes to living in a major city. I lived in goshiwon — buildings packed with tiny rooms just big enough for a bed and a desk, with a shared bathroom at the end of the hall and a communal kitchen — until I got the job in publishing and was able to save up enough to afford the deposit and rent on a semi-basement studio in a small apartment building. While roaming from one marginal housing situation to another on the outskirts of Seoul, I met countless people my age who were just like me. They reminded me of the tiny mammals who cower among the beasts of prey deep in the jungle and must survive on their wits alone.

*

I leave the theatre and march myself straight past all the coffee shops, pubs, and restaurants that line the street. Rush hour has long since ended, so there are plenty of empty seats on the bus. As soon as I sit down, I lean my head against the window and doze off. A sound like a burbling stream keeps rising from my stomach to my chest, startling me awake, but then I drop right back into sleep. When traffic is heavy, it takes over an hour to get from downtown to the new apartment complex that marks the border of the city where I live; at this time of night, it only takes about forty minutes. But I am not headed home to rest just yet.

I wake automatically one stop before my destination, and get off the bus across the intersection from the 24-hour convenience store where I work part-time. I look at the neon store sign while waiting for the crosswalk light to change. The second the light turns green, I break into a sprint, and push open the glass door while still panting for air. I know I'm overplaying it, but the owner is glaring at me. I hurriedly pull on a uniform smock while rattling off apologies.

I'm really, really sorry. I'll stay an extra hour tomorrow morning.

You can't keep missing shift change. What was it? Another play?

Tomorrow's dress rehearsal, then we open the day after.

I don't know why you're wasting your time on something that doesn't even put food on the table. As the owner gets ready to leave, he adds, A delivery arrived, so I left it for you to deal with. See you at 9:00 tomorrow.

He leaves. He will be back in the morning to relieve me, and then his wife will show up whenever she has time during the day so he can take one or two-hour breaks to eat and rest. The part-timers are there to stand vigil in the night while the owners sleep. It is a ten-hour graveyard shift, from 10 p.m. to 8 a.m. There is one other employee, a guy in college, who only works weekends. For me, it's a standard five-day workweek. Working part-time at a convenience store is a lousy way to make money. The hourly pay is the lowest of all the part-time jobs I've held, and for people who don't know what to do with themselves when they are alone, it can be desperately boring. But depending on your situation, having those late-night hours to yourself, to study or read books, can make up for it.

Regardless of location, customers always peter out after midnight. I have actually found that working the graveyard shift suits my schedule best. Before this, I worked at cafés, restaurants, pizza places, hamburger shops, kimbap shops, and once as a parking lot attendant at a department store. Eventually, I discovered that the graveyard shift at a convenience store is perfect for someone like me, because I can do something else during the day in exchange for a little less sleep at night. Though I know that working in theatre is even more pointless than working part-time, it at least gives me the comfort of hope.

At 9 p.m., the dairy products, drinks, and snacks arrive. My first task right after shift change is to shelve the items that have just been delivered. That is also my chance to grab some dinner. After 8 p.m., the pre-packaged sandwiches and triangle kimbap all have to be thrown out. Likewise, the ready-made meals on display have to be pulled before the morning delivery arrives. I remove the rest of the triangle kimbap and ready-made meals that the owner hadn't gotten to yet from the refrigerated display and stack them underneath the counter. Then I refill the shelves with new items. Milk, drinks, and cookies go to the bottom of the stack or to the very back of the row, while the older items are pulled forward. Expiration dates have to be strictly observed. Barcodes are scanned and compostables separated into city-approved trash bags, while expired dairy products, drinks, and snacks are set aside in the storeroom to be returned to the manufacturer.

What should I eat today? I start at the drinks fridge, where several drinks have been grouped with other items as part of a two-plus-one promotion. Customers sometimes leave the freebies behind and take only what they came in for. Banana milk, strawberry milk, chocolate milk, barley tea. I choose a bottle of cornsilk tea. And since I am extra hungry, I grab one of the bigger ready-made meals packed with seven different sides, including sausage, fried pork cutlet, and fishcake. I pop it in the microwave. It is my first proper meal of the day, and a very late dinner at that, since it's already past 10 p.m. I also put four triangle kimbap stuffed with gochujang, tuna, and kimchi into a plastic bag and tuck it away in one of the fridges. That will be my breakfast tomorrow, after I get home. I know it isn't good for me to eat this way, but there is no better method for saving on living expenses. It is also one of the other big advantages to working part-time at a convenience store, despite the low pay. I am so hungry that I wolf the food down and immediately feel sleepy.

I heard that there has been a rash of young people, as exhausted as and not so different from me, going into stores late at night armed with knives and robbing the employees. Ours is a medium-sized convenience store with no ATM and no security cameras. Instead, the owner installed a button under the counter that, when pushed, triggers a loud siren and flashes the lights on and off. He tested it out a few times. Said it was just like a car alarm.

This late at night, we get a few customers dropping by for a midnight snack of chips or noodle cups, or to buy cigarettes, booze, or sodas, but they too thin out around 2 a.m. The delivery trucks make their rounds between 2 and 3 a.m. The timing never varies; they show up at our store close to 3.

I check the order form for the morning delivery that the owner has typed into the computer. After that, there is nothing to do but wait behind the counter, dozing off and waking again over and over, until the delivery truck arrives and I can fill the shelves with new drinks and alcohol, snacks and ready-made meals. Then it is time to clean. I sweep and mop the floor and wash the metal picnic tables and chairs outside. I sort the trash and place it at the collection point on the curb. At 4 a.m., the garbage truck comes by. Afterward, I have another hour and a half to doze off. Sometimes I'm able to get some decent shut-eye that way, but there are still days when I find myself really wishing I could give my lower back a break and lie down flat somewhere. Today is one of those days. And that is how the time passes.

Whenever I look back on the past, everything is so fuzzy. Nothing in particular stands out. Fuck, how did I get so old already? Will things get better if I ever become a famous playwright or director? When I look at friends who are older than me, they don't seem much better off. If anything, they look just as hopeless. As for marriage … I used to fantasise about that from time to time, but the idea of me becoming some man's wife seems as difficult, as impossible even, as achieving my tiny hope of one day being able to have a pet. When I see how my friends are with their pets, when I really think about what it means to have to love something deeply, fuss over it, worry about it, take care of it, keep it close and always be considerate of it, until you grow sick of it and hate it and feel annoyed by it, only to end up fawning over it some more, and petting it and loving it again so much that you can never get rid of it, I feel like I can't breathe. I'll admit that I enjoyed looking after my friend's little white Maltese for ten days while she was on vacation, but I was horrified by how much the dog fawned over whoever took care of it, the way it grovelled. I couldn't deal with that. No way. Even men are too much work now.

Did I ever have any boyfriends worth remembering? There were a couple, though I don't know if I'd say they were really all that memorable. The first was a college classmate, an art major. We were both pretty immature, but he was worse than me. He lived alone in a studio apartment near the school. During my senior year, I didn't have anywhere to live, so I moved in with him. My father had just passed and my uncle was only able to help me with tuition and nothing more. It wasn't long before my boyfriend started suggesting we get married. His parents lived in the countryside and seemed pretty middle-class, but definitely weren't rich. For some reason he kept bugging me to go home with him to meet his parents. I put myself in my father's shoes and imagined asking this boy what his intentions were towards my daughter. What do you plan to do with your life? Sir, I plan to surround myself with beautiful art. I look up at the sky and scoff, then say, What about work? Well, sir, I'm an artist so I guess you could say I'm self-employed. You think you can make a living off of art? In this society?! You deadbeat! Where'll you live? I have a studio, sir. But if it's too small for both of us, then we'll move. I hear those converted rooftop storage sheds aren't bad. You're going to make my daughter and grandchild live in a shed? Get the hell away from my daughter! I dumped him immediately. After we graduated, I joined the theatre group while he went to grad school with help from his family. I bumped into him on the street recently. He said he had a job of some kind, curating maybe, at a small commercial art gallery. Art, theatre. Potato, potahto. It was all one big dead-end. I felt like our relationship was less about romance and more like a game or a passing amusement.

I dated the second guy while working at the publishing house. He was a reporter several years older than me. I figured he was either good with money or got a lot of help from his parents, because he owned his own apartment, around twenty pyeong in size. I wasn't expecting him to be some aspiring investigative journalist, pursuing murder cases or corrupt politicians, the fires of justice burning inside of him, or anything like that. I just took him to be an ordinary salaryman who'd gone to a good college and put on a necktie every morning to go to his perfectly ordinary office. Then he showed up an hour-and-a-half late to one of our dates. He texted me every ten minutes until he got there, and when I finally asked where he'd been, he said he'd been staking out the house of an actress who was on the verge of a divorce. He told me all about the actress's husband and her new lover. It turned out that was what he really did for work. And yet he tried to act like he knew everything about theatre, dropping names like Samuel Beckett and Bertolt Brecht. Later, he went sniffing around all the regular haunts of a pop singer who was embroiled in the middle of a gambling-related scandal, and landed several scoops that way. I got tired of him. I stood him up twice, and he called to swear at me and hung up. I deleted his number.

And then I met Black Shirt. His real name was Kim Minwoo. He was three years older than me and just as poor, but there was something different about him. For him, the worse things got, the fiercer his approach to life. He was like a soldier with his rifle cleaned and loaded, his eyes fixed on some distant spot, his body poised to race forward.

3

My father was fired from his clerical post at the Yeongsan township office during the rapid social upheavals of the 1960s. He was accused of accepting a bribe from someone who'd built an unlicensed building, though I can't say that the bribe did very much for us. Given the state of things at the time, it couldn't have been more than a carton of cigarettes. That was probably the best that a self-taught man who'd never been properly educated could hope for. My father made a couple of scouting trips to Daegu and Seoul, and then sold our shabby country house along with the rice paddies that we'd inherited from my mother's family and moved our family to Seoul.

We unpacked our things in a hillside slum outside of Dongdaemun. It was a monthly rental, a tiny, two-room house built from cinderblocks. There was no yard, and the kitchen door opened directly onto the alley. The windows of both rooms also faced the alley, and the back of the house butted right up against the wall of the neighbouring house. Hanging next to the kitchen door were two keyrings, each of which held a key for the front door and a key for the outhouse. My parents, my little brother, and I had to share those two sets. We also shared the outhouse with our neighbours. To use it, you had to remember to take the keys with you. The outhouse itself faced right onto the street; the wooden plank door was so thin that you could hear people breathing as they walked by while you were doing your business. Though I was young, I still felt embarrassed whenever I ran into someone on my way to and from the bathroom. I can't imagine how much more uncomfortable it must have been for the elders, and especially for my mother.

We had one lifeline in the city: a notary near the district office in Seoul who'd come from the same hometown as my father. He, too, had started out as a minor government employee in the countryside. My father went to work for him as his assistant. The wages my father made were just enough to put food on the table and soju in his glass.

Once we were living in the big city, my mother surprised us with her remarkable flair for making money. She started frequenting Dongdaemun Market and somehow sweet-talked her way into setting up shop right in the middle of a passageway. She peddled socks, underwear, and undershirts.

In my first year of high school, things took a turn. My father had a stroke. He eventually recovered, but his left leg was never the same. Despite that setback, we somehow managed to make ends meet.

We left the hillside slum near Dongdaemun and moved to Dalgol, or Moon Hollow, which turned out to be much worse. It was not yet a proper neighbourhood. Everyone there either had been living near Jungnang Stream and Chonggye Stream before being pushed out by developers or had spilled over from the other slum right across the street. Running water was only available at a public tap in an empty lot, and since there were many houses without indoor plumbing, shared outhouses were clustered along the main road. Our house had two rooms and a longish, skinny yard that ran the length of the narrow, wrap-around porch, and the location wasn't bad: just over the block wall was the roof of the house down the slope from ours, the rest of the neighbourhood, and even a view of downtown in the distance. But best of all, we had our own private outhouse. We were so far uphill that we didn't get running water until I graduated from high school. Though it was a shabby house with wooden boards instead of glass in the windows, my mother had bravely taken out a loan in order to pay the jeonse deposit, a large lump sum that we would get back at the end of our rental contract.

A market had been forming near the entrance to Moon Hollow, and my mother acquired the right to set up shop there. She knew that no one would be interested in buying underthings in a slum market and figured she'd do far better with food, so she poured her heart into the arduous task of selling fish. She started out buying seafood wholesale at the Dongdaemun Fish Market to sell in our neighbourhood. The most she could handle were a few crates of mackerel, saury, hairtail, and pollack that she would display on her tiny stand; whenever customers came, she cleaned and gutted the fish for them. While the rest of us were fast asleep, my mother would rise at dawn to fetch her wares. As the market grew, vendors chipped in funds for their own cargo truck, which meant less hardship and more goods to sell. It was around that same time that my father began working for her.

None of us thought that my father, who'd worked behind a desk all his life and was now crippled, to boot, would be of any help at my mother's fish stand. But to our surprise, he took the fish that didn't sell and turned it into eomuk, savoury strips of deep-fried fishcake. He used soy meal that he got from the tofu vendor across the street and added it to the ground-up fish meat, then mixed it with a little starch; the result tasted better and was more nutritious than fishcake made with flour. Pretty much every single person in Moon Hollow was a fan of our fishcake. My father researched and experimented on his own to come up with different types of delicious fishcake, and many was the day that we sold out and had to close shop early. It was a natural transition from fishmonger to fishcake vendor. That was how my parents spent the next dozen or so years, making a living at the Moon Hollow market. The rental house became our house, my parents bought themselves a proper shop, and sent me and my brother to university. They never actually made enough to buy a middle-class house, though.

But I didn't depend entirely on my parents. After we moved to Seoul, I threw myself headlong into studying. There wasn't much to do besides study, but also, I was determined to get out of the slum. I was admitted into a top-ranked university, where I did what a few of my other classmates were doing and worked part-time as a tutor, until I lucked into becoming a live-in tutor for a wealthy family, which enabled me to move out of my parents' house. After completing my army service, I continued to live on my own, and later studied abroad. I didn't live with my parents until marriage like other people did.

*

When did I first meet Jaemyung? I guess it was the summer vacation of my first year of high school, just a few months after we'd moved to Moon Hollow. From the big, three-way intersection at the entrance, where the marketplace was, the main road led uphill, right through the middle. Countless alleyways branched off it on both sides. But not all of the streets were alleys; there were also paved two-lane roads that led to four-way intersections, with public taps or toilets or small shops filling out the corners. Our house was in an alley to the right of the third intersection. Jaemyung lived at the end of a narrow alley on the other side of the intersection. Though we called his the last house, the road didn't actually stop there but continued uphill, narrowing into a steep path topped off by a staircase hewn from stones dug from the mountain. Before getting to know Jaemyung's family, I never had any reason to venture up his alley. Usually, after helping my parents out in the market, I would follow the main road back, past the public tap and the toilets, and turn at the corner tobacco shop into our own alley.

Whenever I trudged down to the market in the evenings, a group of four or five raggedy-looking boys would often be standing at the entrance to Jaemyung's alley. A few of them would be smoking. Each time I passed them, I'd feel an odd tug at the back of my head and would turn to look, only to be met with one of the smoking boys saying, What're you lookin' at, man? But then one day, one of them snatched my school uniform hat right off.

Give it back.

Got any money?

I said give it back.

Ha! Look at the glare in his eyes!

Just then, from the dark alley came a shrill voice, yelling, Hey, give him his hat back! The owner of the voice was — to put it in the same terms those boys back then would have used — no taller than a dick. He was so short and stout that I was practically looking down at him. He grabbed my hat from the other boy and handed it to me. Let's box sometime, he said. I took my hat and walked away without responding. The kid was none other than Jaemyung's younger brother. His real name was Jaegeun, but since he was the youngest and the shortest, he'd ended up stuck with the nickname 'Jjaekkan', which meant 'runt' in their southern dialect. The rest of the group all worked as shoeshine boys for Jaemyung; there were ten of them in total.

On warm summer evenings, the whole neighbourhood would pour out into the street, the grown-ups doing their own thing — men gathered in clusters to drink and play janggi, women sitting in circles with their skirts or pant legs hitched up just above their knees, cackling and gossiping — while the smaller kids raised a ruckus, playing games of tag and red light, green light. The kids like me, teenagers who were neither grown-up nor child, either ganged up and headed downhill or hiked up to the peak to get some fresh air. Our house was close to the top of the hill. All I had to do was turn right at the end of the main road and hike up the path to the top, where a few trees still remained and the grass grew thick. From above, I could see another neighbourhood on the other side of the hill, the lights in their windows glowing against the night sky. I could also see Mt Bukhan, and beyond that, the red neon glow of downtown spreading to the horizon. At the very top of our hill were a few boulders, and below those, a wide open space.

I climbed to the peak one day to find a group of kids and even a few adults cheering and hooting as they watched some sort of fight. I sat on a boulder and watched, too. I don't know where they'd found them, but two of the guys were wearing boxing gloves and going at each other. Duck! Yeah, in, out. Extend that arm, man! Jab, jab, uppercut! That's right! One of the guys got knocked down hard, and the referee-slash-coach called a time-out.

You. Come here.

The winner called me over. It was the same boy who'd challenged me to a fight a few days earlier.

You're the schoolkid who just moved in up the hill from us, right? Want to spar?

I didn't want to, but I was no coward either. I joined the group, feeling bashful, but also a little proud that he'd acknowledged my existence. I was no fighter, but after moving to the slums outside of Dongdaemun, I'd had my share of run-ins with all sorts of characters. Back then, the primary schools were overcrowded: there were over twenty different classes per grade, and the student body was divided into a morning shift and an afternoon shift. Middle school wasn't as bad, but there were still at least a dozen classes with over seventy or eighty students in each class. When I first got there, I was bullied for being a hick, but I learned from it. I learned that if anyone messed with me, I absolutely could not back down. I had to fight every day, no matter how overpowered or outnumbered I was, until my opponents gave up. No one ever took pity on the loser. If I lost a fight, then I challenged the kid to a rematch after school the next day, and the day after that, I waited in front of his house to challenge him again, and again, until he finally begged for mercy. I could not stop until he apologised or begged me to stop. There was no point in running home to Mummy and Daddy; neither of them gave a shit if my lip was busted or nose broken. Besides, I had to look out for my younger brother; I couldn't expect anyone to look out for me. That was why I did not back down from Jjaekkan's challenge. I knew all too well how hellish my life in that neighbourhood would be if I did.

While Jjaekkan, who'd already gotten the taste of one victory, danced around, tapping his gloves together, I held my hands out politely so the referee could put the other pair of gloves on me. I stood there awkwardly, wearing boxing gloves for the first time in my life. The referee gave us a pat on the back and said, Go! Instantly, I saw stars. I learned later that it was called a straight jab. Luckily, I'd boxed just enough to know to put my head down, my fists up, and to start moving. I threw a punch, and Jjaekkan dodged it easily and returned it with a jab. I took several more hits. If you get mad, you lose, I muttered to myself, and grit my teeth. Then Jjaekkan socked me right in the face, and I staggered, my nose streaming with blood. I crouched, came in close, and swung my fist up hard in an uppercut. My glove hit something solid and heavy. Jjaekkan fell on his ass. He sprang back up, danced around, and came towards me again.

Hey, that's enough.

The referee separated us. My nose was still bleeding, staining the front of my undershirt. That's a lot of blood, the ref muttered, and wiped my face with the towel slung over his shoulder. I caught a strong whiff of sweat.

It's only round one. Why'd you stop us? Jjaekkan panted.

It's a draw! You fell on your arse, and he's bleeding.

Jjaekkan must have figured that my busted nose meant he'd saved enough face, because he stopped arguing and took off his gloves.

Tell your parents you got that while exercising, the referee said. I'm guessing this wasn't your first match?

I told him it was.

That's one hell of an uppercut for your first match. You've got talent. What's your name?

Park Minwoo.

I'm Jaemyung. You can call me Hyung. Hey, Jaegeun, this guy's name is Minwoo. Shake.

We awkwardly shook hands.

I was impressed by Jaemyung's handling of the situation. He smoothly accepted me as one of the neighbourhood boys without hurting anyone's pride.

I ended up being really tight with Jaemyung and

his brothers, up until my second year in high school. Jaemyung was twenty, and the middle son. The oldest was Jaesup, who must've been around twenty-two at the time. Every few months, Jaesup would return home and stay for a few weeks before disappearing again. Jjaekkan, who was one year older than me, was the third son. He was the youngest of the boys, but the true youngest of the family was Myosoon, the only girl. She was two or three years younger than me.

They had no father. Jaemyung was effectively the man of the house. His mother and Myosoon took care of the housekeeping, while Jaemyung earned a living by managing shoeshine stands in front of Hyundae Theatre, Manseok Grill House, and Hometown Coffeeshop. All of the brothers had dropped out after a few years of primary school. Jjaekkan proudly referred to himself and his brothers as Third Grade, Fourth Grade, and Fifth Grade. When I asked which of them had made it all the way to the fifth grade, I was not surprised to learn it was clever Jaemyung. They added that their father, who'd been a farmer, had passed away immediately after moving the family up from Jeolla Province, but even if he had lived, he still wouldn't have had the means to keep all of the boys in school.

During that summer vacation, I spent two or three evenings every week at the top of the hill. I was determined to learn how to box from Jaemyung. He taught me proper footwork, to stand with one foot forward and shift my weight back and forth, to generate power from my legs, to keep my head down and use my fists and elbows to protect my face, my sides, my stomach, while throwing punches, uppercuts, hooks, and jabs. Though we had no gym equipped with sandbags, I practiced my breathing and strengthened my body and agility by doing things like jumping rope and running in place.

After dropping out of primary school, Jaemyung had gone to work for someone else's shoeshine stand on Jongno Street downtown, working his way up through the various ranks, from jjiksae, the lowest-ranked boys who fetched shoes from customers, to ddaksae, the ones who cleaned the shoes, and finally gwangsae, the ones who actually shined them. He started boxing as a way to defend himself. He figured out early on that real fights were different from sparring in class, so he worked on perfecting a repertoire of techniques, taking hapkido for half a year, judo for three or four months, and boxing for a year. He learned how to instantly recognise an opponent's individual fighting style. He said that he was invincible even against martial artists with advanced belts who'd been through scores of matches. The owner of the boxing gym recognised Jaemyung's skills in the ring and put him through intense training to try to debut him as a professional boxer.

Why'd you quit? I asked.

Jaemyung chuckled and said, That's when Supsup was thrown in the clink. Someone had to put food on the table.

'Supsup' was their nickname for their oldest brother Jaesup. That was how I learned that Jaesup was an ex-con. He'd been put away for stealing. Every few months he would show up at home, stash stolen record players or television sets in the cramped room where the boys slept, and make a nuisance of himself before selling off the goods and disappearing again. Jaemyung said that Jaesup had recently joined a company, since being a company man was safer and paid better. I asked what kind of company would take someone with no schooling, but Jaemyung explained that 'company' was what they called a team of pickpockets.

Relax your shoulders, and your arms, too. When you move in — bam! bam! — that's when you clench. Got it? My coach used to use this one word all the time, like the something-ship, maybe agro-ship, agro-ship. You're studying English, so you know it.

I had no idea what he was saying at first, but after racking my brain to think of an English word that sounded similar, I realised the word was 'aggressive'.

The first time I went with Jjaekkan to his house, I was surprised. It was just like all the other houses in the neighbourhood, with walls made from cinderblocks patched over with cement, and it had no yard or toilet and butted right up against the street, but it was big, twice the size of my family's house. They'd knocked out a wall between two small houses that had been built against each other and turned it into one decently sized house. There was one large room, two smaller rooms, and even a spacious breezeway in the middle. The dozen or so shoeshine boys all slept in the big room, Myosoon and their mother slept in the room next to the kitchen, and Jaemyung and Jjaekkan slept in the other small room. The back of the breezeway faced the hillside, which had been reinforced for the house uphill from theirs, the eaves of which hung low and kept their home in shadow. But they had a large clay jar that the children took turns refilling with water from the public tap and used to wash their faces and keep their hands and feet clean.

At dinner time, they placed a long table fashioned from wooden planks in the breezeway; as soon as Jaemyung sat, the rest of the children filled both sides of the table. I sat across from Jaemyung, and Jjaekkan sat beside him. Their mother ladled up bowls of sujebi that she'd cooked in a large pot, while Myosoon carried the bowls from the kitchen to the table. Once Myosoon and their mother were seated at the end of the table, dinner began. Instead of the usual firm dough torn by hand, their sujebi was made with a runny dough that was scraped with a pair of chopsticks into a pot of boiling water; as you ate it, the dough flakes quickly turned soggy and loose until you were basically eating flour porridge. The flour must have been of poor quality to begin with, as it was yellowish in colour, and the broth wasn't made from beef or anchovy stock but was just plain water with a little soy sauce and sliced squash. It barely qualified as sujebi. To my surprise, a single bowl of white rice was placed in front of Jaemyung. His mother, Myosoon, and Jjaekkan all got sujebi, but he was served a proper meal of rice and kimchi. Of course, the kimchi wasn't the properly fermented kind, but rather a handful of outer cabbage leaves salted and sprinkled with a bit of ground red pepper. Jaemyung lifted his spoon and hesitated, then offered me his rice.

Since you're our guest, maybe you should eat this instead.

No sooner was the offer out than I felt the sharp stares of the other children. My hair stood on end.

No thanks, I like sujebi.

With that, Jaemyung ate a huge spoonful of the rice, and everyone turned back to their own bowls. Rice was a sacred privilege afforded only to the head of the household responsible for keeping the family alive. That image has stayed with me ever since.

*

At my family's shop, any of the fishcakes that came out of the deep fryer torn or with rounded corners were plucked out with tongs by my father and tossed to one side of the prep table. My father made the dough for the fishcakes, while two older girls who worked at the shop moulded the dough. They scooped just the right amount into shallow, square moulds, smoothed out the top, and gave the moulds a tap to release perfect squares of dough into the hot oil. I marveled at how smooth and mechanical their movements were. The cooked fishcakes would float to the top of the oil, a delicious golden-brown, and my father would scoop them out and place the sellable ones to the left and toss the torn ones to the right. My mother's job was to count the cakes and either stack them or box them up for orders, and to handle customers. A large fan for cooling the deep-fried fishcakes rattled away all day long.

When my younger brother and I got home from school, we snacked on the torn fishcakes, still warm from the fryer. Once our hunger was sated, we'd laugh and point at each other's greasy mouths. My mother would wrap up the rest of the torn fishcake from that day and send us out to deliver them to places she owed favours to or anywhere else that she needed to stay on the good side of. That meant places like the tiny shack inhabited by the elderly man who fetched water from the public tap for us and the other vendors in the marketplace, the garbage collectors' station, the police box, and so on. Every now and then, we delivered fishcake to Jaemyung's family, too; those days were feasts for the shoeshine boys. Because of that, my brother and I came to have some status in our neighbourhood. Grown-ups would strike up conversation with us first, asking where we were going and whether we were on our way back from school, and whenever one of us showed up on someone's doorstep right around the time dinner preparations were beginning, the woman of the house would welcome us with a huge smile and tell us how much easier we'd just made her day.

In his spare time, our father filled out government forms for fellow marketplace vendors, as well as for other people in the neighbourhood who'd heard about his skills. I didn't find out until later, but we were not nicknamed the 'fishcake house' as would have been customary, but rather the 'scholar house'. I was one of the only two high school students in our neighbourhood at the time. The other was Cha Soona, the noodle-house daughter. Her family lived near the public tap, to the left of the first intersection, down the hill from Jaemyung's house and mine.

Back then, rice was in short supply, and the government was waging a campaign to encourage people to eat more flour and mixed grains. At school, our lunchboxes were inspected daily, and anyone caught bringing white rice had their palms strapped. Flour, donated as food aid by the United States and stamped on each sack with a picture of a handshake, was distributed by the neighbourhood office and eventually found its way into the marketplace. Lunch in every home consisted of sujebi, knife-cut noodles, or banquet noodles — the extra-thin soup noodles that were extruded by machine and so insubstantial that you'd barely even chewed them before they were slipping down your throat. They were called banquet noodles because we used to eat them only on special days, but they were ubiquitous in our neighbourhood since you could prepare them many different ways, including in soup or tossed in a spicy sauce. What made it even better was cooking the noodles in a broth made from meat or anchovy stock with a handful of sliced fishcake. That was as good as a holiday meal for the neighbourhood kids. Of course, my brother and I quickly grew sick of fishcake, but it was still a decent replacement for meat. Fishcakes and noodle soup were the favourites of the people in our neighbourhood.

It hadn't been long since we'd started selling fishcake, so I'm thinking this was right around the autumn of my second year in high school. My mother had wrapped up the leftover fishcake in newspaper and told me to take it to the noodle house. My heart immediately began to race. I knew Soona and had bumped into her several times on the way to and from school. You'd have to be new to the neighbourhood or possibly intellectually disabled to be a teenager living there and *not* know Soona. Besides, her house was right in front of the tap, where everyone in the neighbourhood got their water. The sight of her, walking down the market street to the bus stop every morning in her school uniform, the white collar stiffly ironed, her hair in two long braids, was like sighting a single white crane in the middle of a disaster area. She was beautiful, eye-catching even at a distance. She had these big eyes, fair skin, a pretty nose, and a certain primness in her expression. A smile is nice, but the truth is, it's the girls who seem a little coy and standoffish, the unapproachable girls, that really drive boys crazy. That was Jjaekkan's take, Jaemyeong's opinion, and my feeling, too. None of us ever let on, but we were all in love with Soona.

I wrapped up the fishcake and rushed toward the public tap in my excitement, but I slowed as I got closer. For some reason, I suddenly felt ashamed of the fishcake wrapped in newspaper. I felt like everyone standing near the tap would take one look at the grease stains on the paper and know what I was carrying. Overwhelmed by a sense of inferiority, I muttered to myself, That's the best you can do? Just this leftover fishcake? I arrived at her house. It had a square sign over it that said 'Noodles' and a piece of paper taped to the glass door that said, 'We sell noodle soup.' I assumed the neat handwriting belonged to her.

The door opened onto a large room with a noodle machine; a belt and pulley system kept it turning. Outside, a drying rack as high as the courtyard wall was covered with noodles. Whenever I walked past the public tap, I could see them taking noodles off the rack and hanging new ones. Just inside the door, to the right, were bundles of dried noodles, wrapped in paper and stacked on a mat. I'd been there before to buy those very bundles.

I opened the door and stepped inside, but no one was around. I called out to see if anyone was home, and Soona stuck her head out of a door further in. She nodded, as if she recognised me. She came out to greet me and picked up one of the bundles of noodles. I caught a scent of something sweet.

Uh, I said, I didn't come to buy noodles … Here.

She immediately recognised the package of fishcakes.

Oh, delicious!

She smiled at me, the straight line of her teeth showing through her lips. That smile was like a punch to the chest. My chest ached and I felt breathless.

Thank you, she said.

I had nothing to say in return so I turned to leave, but she stopped me.

Wait, please take this in exchange.

She offered me the noodles again. I took them without thinking and regretted it the moment I was out the door. Since it wasn't offered to me by her parents, I should have refused. But how could I say no to her? I tucked the noodles under my arm and ran home for fear of being seen, my face bright red the whole way.

To me, high school girls were creatures I saw all the time on the bus to and from school, but for the kids of the neighbourhood who couldn't afford to go to school, they must have looked like unclimbable trees. Once, I'd dropped by Jaemyung's house in my school uniform, and bumped into Myosoon as she was coming out of the kitchen.

Oh, my! Minwoo, you're so handsome! Look at that

uniform. You look like something out of a movie.

And this part I still remember like it was yesterday: I knew then that they would all be out of my life one day soon. That was why, deep down, I believed I had to do right by them, no matter what. I suppose I'd been feeling that way ever since I'd first met Jjaekkan and his shoeshine boys.

*

Jaemyung had the corner on the best spots in town for his shoeshine stands; his territory was highly coveted. Clever, skillful Jaemyung ran the stands well. He befriended the manager of the Hyundae Theatre, who painted the movie posters, and the projectionist, and later, with their help, negotiated the rights to the space out front with the theatre owner, paying him a lump sum as street tax. Every neighbourhood had its share of gangs, but Jaemyung had fought to establish his place in the pecking order from the get-go, and had earned their respect. Though the 'Three-way Intersection Gang' across the street was the strongest, they were all friends of friends, so they left him alone.

The second location, in front of Manseok Grill House, was in the alley next to the theatre. Jaemyung and his boys had taken turns keeping the restaurant clean both inside and out and shooing away peddlers and panhandlers, for which they naturally earned the right to set up shop outside. As for Hometown Coffeeshop, that was right at the entrance to the Moon Hollow marketplace, on the first floor of a three-storey building. The location was great, and it was always bustling with customers since there were plenty of passers-by. But being right on the main street made it a little hard to set up a shoeshine stand directly outside. So Jaemyung set up shop in an alley nearby instead, complete with a tarp roof, like a food cart. Jaemyung spent most of his time in front of Hyundae Theatre and kept an eye on the Grill House, while Jjaekkan took three of the boys with him to work at the Hometown Coffeeshop location. Thanks to Jaemyung, I was able to see all the good movies for free at the Hyundae. All he had to do was nod to the ticket taker while giving me a little shove through the entrance, and I was in.

One day a fight broke out at Hometown. Jjaekkan was cleaning shoes with the ddaksae, when the jjiksae he'd sent to fetch shoes from the coffeeshop came back with a busted lip. Some newcomers had set up chairs right outside the coffeeshop and were shining shoes. They'd stopped the jjiksae from even entering the coffeeshop and had thrashed him right in the doorway. The ddaksae boys were ready to rush right over, but Jjaekkan stopped them and went to see for himself. Just as the runner had said, two chairs had been set up for receiving customers, and there were several pair of shoes that had been fetched from customers inside the coffeeshop. Three boys were squatting on the ground, cleaning the shoes. Jjaekkan approached them. But he did not waste his time with asking where they had come from or who told them to work there, or with warning them that the spot was taken.

You beat my kid? was all he said.

One of the boys, who was even shorter and stouter than little Jjaekkan, scowled until a deep furrow formed on his brow, and stood.

Find somewhere else to work, he said. This is our turf now.

Jjaekkan was so dumbfounded that all he could say in return was, Since when?

We got permission from the building owner, the boy said arrogantly.

Jjaekkan chuckled and turned to leave. He knew all too well how Jaemyung handled kids like these, so he didn't bother dealing with him head-on.

It took Jaemyung and Jjaekkan less than a day to find out who the kid was. The kid's nickname was 'Tomak', which meant 'stump', and he was one year younger than Jjaekkan, which made him the same age as me. He'd moved there two months earlier from another neighbourhood in the shadow of the mountains. It was right across from ours, so he knew some of the kids in the Three-way Intersection Gang already. They said he was a black belt in taekwondo. A taekwondo studio had opened on the second floor of the Hometown Coffeeshop building just a few months earlier.

The master was a third-degree black belt, about three or four years older than Jaemyung. Tomak was teaching taekwondo to younger kids there as well. That was how he'd recruited several of them to work at his shoeshine stands so he could make money on the side. Jaemyung came to an immediate decision.

Fuck it. Drop the coffeehouse.

What? Are you crazy?

Jjaekkan was livid. I couldn't help butting in either.

That's a bad idea, I said. Word will get out that he pushed you around.

There's no point in rushing this, Jaemyung said. Jjaekkan, starting tomorrow, collect shoes from the other shops near the three-way intersection.

We were unhappy about it but didn't argue with him. When there was no return fire, Tomak grew even bolder and came to Jjaekkan's new location to extort whatever coins he could take from the ddaksae. Finally, Jjaekkan blew up at Jaemyung.

What're you, scared? If we say nothing, we'll get eaten alive.

The children of Moon Hollow all knew better than to cross Jaemyung, and the power he held had earned him the prime spots along the main road. But with Tomak's appearance, the power balance shifted, and gangs of younger kids, seven or eight at a time, began to circle. I'd been around my share of slum children while living outside Dongdaemun and in Moon Hollow. They pretty much raised themselves. They would drop out of school early and gang up to work as street peddlers or thieves, and when they got a little bit older, they went to work in factories. Most left home permanently when it was time to do their military service.

As luck would have it, Jaesup came home just a few months later and heard all about the changes to the neighbourhood from Jjaekkan. The second Jaemyung got home from shining shoes, Jaesup grilled him about it.

I'm just trying to stay out of trouble, Jaemyung protested. A taekwondo master won't be easy to beat, so I'm biding my time.

Are you kidding me? Are you not Jaemyung, younger brother of Supsup? What'd you study all that hapkido, judo, and boxing for? How do you expect to make a living this way? We're going there first thing tomorrow and ripping him a new one.

The next day, the two brothers took three of the older ddaksae boys with them and headed downhill to the market. When they got to Hometown Coffeeshop, the shoeshine boys out front told them that Tomak was in the middle of teaching a beginners' taekwondo class. They all ran upstairs. The master had left Tomak in charge and was out running errands. The ddaksae ignored Tomak, who was in the middle of barking out a series of *hi-yah!*s, and chased the students out of the room.

Nice to finally meet you, arsehole.

As Jaemyung clenched his fists, Tomak assumed an attack position, sliding his feet into place.

Let's get this over with.

Look at you! Trying to act tough.

Jaemyung ducked to avoid Tomak's roundhouse kick and socked him hard in the side and twice on the jaw. Tomak fell.

So much for your black belt. Get up, you little shit.

Jaemyung hauled Tomak up by the collar and punched him in the stomach with a right hook. Tomak curled up like a shrimp and writhed on the floor. The whole time, Jaesup was tearing the mirrors off the wall and smashing picture frames and whatever else he could find. Jaemyung finished with a warning.

I hear you ripped off my boys? I've been trying to look the other way, but no more. I know where you live. I know where your dad works. I'm nice, so I'll let you have the coffeehouse. But if you take so much as one step away from there, I will ruin you. So watch it.

They left Tomak curled up on the broken glass and left. They figured the master would come looking for them as soon as he saw what had happened.

Up the main road through the centre of town and past the intersection near my house, the paved road ended and split into two paths, one of which was the stone staircase. The other path wound around, leading eventually to the top of the hill, but the staircase went straight up to the peak. Right before the peak was a clearing where someone had tried to put in a planted field but gave up. From there, you could see the whole neighbourhood and beyond, all the way down to City Hall. In some spots, you could even see some of the new alleyways and right into people's yards. The top of the hill was frequented by everyone, young and old alike, but this abandoned field was ours alone. We assumed Tomak would know where to find us. When the sun was on the verge of sinking, the lookout warned us that they were coming. Jaesup and Jaemyung sat at a janggi board, while the rest of us stood around. Tomak was the first to appear along the path, followed by his muscular taekwondo master.

Who did it? Which of you arseholes smashed up my studio?

Jaesup waved him over.

You're the master? Come sit with me.

Jaemyung stood to clear a spot for him. Tomak's master didn't hesitate, despite the rest of us standing there. He walked straight over. Jaesup remained seated at the janggi board.

I don't mind fighting you, but hear me out first.

The master was red in the face, fists clenched, as if ready to rush at him that second.

We don't need to talk, arsehole.

As he took a step closer, Jaesup waved his arms.

C'mon now, just listen for a second! I mean, hear me out. Let's say this is the shoeshine stand, and this is the taekwondo studio.

He set two janggi pieces on the board with a loud clack. Tomak's master bent over without thinking, to get a closer look at the board, and instantly Jaesup was on his feet and driving his knee into the master's face. With a *puck!* we heard his nose break, and he staggered at the sudden attack. Jaesup grabbed his hair with both hands and drove his knee into his face over and over. Tomak and the two other boys he'd brought with him could only stand and stare, too caught off guard to react. Jaesup dragged the master, now passed out and bloodied, by his armpits and dropped him at the edge of the hill.

Call the cops on me if you want. But when you move into someone else's neighbourhood, you better play nice, you piece of shit. You think it's a game, with those little buddies of yours? Behave yourself and stick to teaching taekwondo, before someone decides to burn that studio down.

With that, he kicked the limp taekwondo master down the side of the hill like he was kicking away a rag. The master rolled and slid until he came to a stop face-down on the road. He never budged.

Word of what happened spread instantly, not only through our neighbourhood, but across the three-way intersection to the neighbouring village as well. The scandal grew: people were saying that he'd lost ten teeth top and bottom, that his nose had caved in, that he spent eight weeks in the hospital. A detective from the local police station came to see Jaesup and Jaemyung. The taekwondo master ended up losing even more face, for not only losing a fight but also telling the police.

Witnessing all of this made me think about how cutthroat life can be. I figured that our tiny hell was a miniature version of the world outside. By the time I started my third year of high school, I was absolutely certain that I had to decide on a path for myself, that I had to fight my way out of there. I'd started noticing girls around then, too, but I concentrated solely on studying for the college entrance exam, determined to get out of the slum any way I could.

By the time I figured out that nearly all of the boys in the neighbourhood had a crush on Soona, the noodle-house girl, I was already deeply in love with her. The first sign was when Jjaekkan took over the chore of filling the water jar at his house. When I praised him for being so diligent, the shoeshine boys all glanced at each other and snickered.

Jaemyung said, Why do you think he's doing it? He just wants to get a look at Soona.

Of course, I thought. The public tap was right next to the noodle house.

Then Jaemyung went to the noodle house himself and glued a movie poster from the Hyundae Theatre on the door and presented Soona with a pair of movie tickets.

71

And according to Jjaekkan, Tomak was going there every couple of days to buy noodles. I'd noticed that they were eating more noodles than sujebi at Jaemyung's place, but had thought it meant they were making more money than usual. Even Myosoon seemed to notice the change in her brothers, because she threw a fit one day, crying that she wanted to go to school, too, like Soona.

Every now and then, I'd spot Soona in the distance while going to or from school, and sometimes we ended up on the same bus together. One day, I boarded the bus to see her sitting right in front of me. She offered to hold my bag as I stood. I smiled bashfully and nodded, but didn't say a word. Maybe it was because we were the only two students in our neighbourhood, but she wasn't shy about striking up a conversation with me.

Oh, you got this from the North Seoul Library, she said.

One of the books had slid out of my bag.

You go there, too? I asked happily.

Of course, that's where I check out my books …

We ran out of things to say after that. Once we got off the bus, we'd be in the market and would have to pretend not to know each other. As our stop got closer, I started to get nervous.

So, uh, I began. I'm going there on Friday. Would you like to go together?

After school? What time?

Around 4:30?

Sounds good.

The library was about halfway between my school and Soona's school. It was open until six, which gave us ample time. As luck would have it, it rained that Friday. I deliberately left the house without an umbrella just so I could share hers. She and I hung out together a few more times after that, and during the few free months we had after the college entrance exam, I often invited her to hang out with me downtown. Strangely enough, my memories of her from that time are all jumbled together and disconnected. But I guess that's only natural, since I've been living in a different world in the decades since.

4

The morning begins with a cacophony of sounds, each one scrambling to outdo the other and setting my nerves on edge. I doze off during the lull in customers and jump in alarm at the sound of the door opening. The noise of passing cars, which I usually don't even notice, fills my head. I've been getting so little sleep lately and running around so much during the day, what with rehearsals and preparations for opening night that it's harder than usual to get through the hour of overtime. Each time I shake my head to chase away sleep, I feel like I'm poking a beehive, like a swarm of bees is flying around my skull and blocking everything from sight. Whenever I feel this completely exhausted, I think about Kim Minwoo of the black shirt. For a while, whenever I saw a guy on the street walking along in a black shirt and baseball cap, my stomach would sink, and just the sound of a pizza delivery scooter could make my insides churn with nausea. I remember how he introduced himself to me for the first time. Hi, I'm laid-off.

What? I said. Your name is Laid Off? What kind of name is that? I laughed at my own joke, but he didn't react in the slightest and simply repeated, No, I mean I was laid off.

I met him while working part-time at a pizza place. It wasn't one of those things where you fall for a customer while serving them pizza. He worked there, too. Other than the manager, everyone who worked there was in their twenties, but he stuck out. He looked older than the others, like the guys who appear at the start of a new college semester after having been on leave to complete their mandatory two years of military service. It turned out he was thirty-one, and working as a delivery driver. He always wore a black shirt. The text or pictures on the front varied, and the sleeve length and thickness changed with the seasons, but otherwise it was black shirts all year round. I'm pretty sure I was the first to ever ask him why he wore only black. His answer, as always, was simple: Because I hate doing laundry. So the employees all took to calling him Black Shirt instead of Minwoo. But he and I weren't that close when we worked there. We may as well have been strangers.

I guess the manager saw that I was healthy and energetic because he immediately put me to work helping out in the kitchen. I wasn't allowed to make the dough, but I took care of the toppings and prepped the ingredients. I messed up a few times by mixing up orders and was immediately put on probation. That meant my hourly wages were docked for three months. I'd heard that even part-time jobs were supposed to come with employment contracts, but the manager had never mentioned one, and I let the matter go because I assumed it was just common practice to pay your workers as promised. I memorised all of the pizza recipes in the first month and waited patiently through the remaining two months of probation. Then, in the fourth month, I got my paycheck and saw that I was still on probation pay. When I asked the manager about it, he said that I'd inconvenienced him by taking two days off in the middle. I said, okay, but wasn't docking 300,000 won from my pay a little much, and he countered by threatening to extend my probation. I was powerless. A single adult living in Seoul needs 1,600,000 won to get by; I was barely making half of the 1,000,000 won I'd been promised. That meant my hourly wage was only 3,000 won.

As I was arguing with the manager and on the verge of quitting right then and there, Black Shirt stopped me. He asked the manager why he'd never offered me an employment contract and pointed out that it was illegal not to do so. He checked off the things the manager had done wrong: if there was a three-month probation, then I should have been informed of that when I was first hired, and once the probation period was up, I should have been paid my full hourly rate. But the manager claimed that it was not his fault and that I'd accepted the conditions, and proceeded to ignore us. Black Shirt slowly took off the uniform top printed with the store logo and said he was quitting, too, and that he would report the manager to the Ministry of Employment and Labor and to the neighbourhood Employment Information Centre the very next day. The manager snorted and said, Knock yourself out, and just like that, he and I both quit.

Since then, of course, I've pretty much given up. As long as the work and the hourly rate are reasonable, I don't argue. The convenience store only pays 4,500 won an hour, though in my case, I should be making time and a half because I work the night shift plus overtime. Also, if I work a five-day week, I'm supposed to get an extra day's worth of pay for working on my day off. But instead I agreed to a flat 60,000 won for a ten-hour graveyard shift. In exchange, I get paid in cash at the end of every shift. Just a few years ago, I would never have stood for such injustice and would not have been satisfied until I'd quibbled over every little thing, but now the thought of doing that just seems like a bother, so I settled for a reasonable compromise.

A few days after quitting the pizza place, I was in the middle of a rehearsal at the theatre when I got a message that someone had come to see me. It was Black Shirt. He gave me a ride in his ancient Galloper jeep with its noisy engine back to the pizza place. The owner was waiting to hand us envelopes filled with 300,000 in won. I cracked open the envelope and gave the bills a quick count, then folded it in half and started to shove it into my back pocket. Black Shirt grabbed it from me.

You make it too easy for someone to steal it. Put it in your bag.

I was excited about the sudden windfall and couldn't bring myself to just walk away after what he'd done for me, so I said, Let's go celebrate!

He looked around and led me to a place nearby that served blood-sausage soup. As we walked inside, he muttered, Girls these days have a lot of growing up to do.

I asked how this miracle had transpired. It turned out that he hadn't reported it to the Ministry of Employment and Labor or to the Employment Information Centre. He knew all too well that, despite the laws, not only would they not bother trying to get such a small amount of money from the business owners, they would never even notify them. Instead, he had a friend call the manager and say in an intimidating voice that the company had been hit with charges and ask why the manager was causing problems. Then, he made a picket sign the size of a door, printed with large block letters, and stood in front of the pizza shop, from the lunchtime rush all the way through until dinnertime. At last, he was contacted by the pizza chain owner himself, who was usually at another shop. He said the owner came in person, looked into the situation, and offered a settlement. He told me the next time I took a job, even if it was for part-time wages, I had to make sure I had an employment contract. That it was the only way to ensure the length of my employment, my working hours, my job description, and the appropriate wages.

Within the week, he helped me find a new job at a coffeeshop near the university. He told me he used to work for a large construction company. After losing his job there, he'd been getting by on two or three part-time jobs at a time. I met up with him now and then. Usually, he came to see me as I was getting off work, and when the play I was directing opened, I invited him to the theatre. We were becoming such good friends that other people started mistaking us as a longtime couple. But we both knew that neither of us were in any position for fooling around or dating, and so we maintained an unspoken but careful distance. There was definitely a vibe between us whenever we were alone, but we both ignored it and just enjoyed each other's company. Sometimes, when we met over soju to gripe with each other, I'd get a sudden urge to cry, and would stare at the words or picture printed on the front of his black shirt then make a quick joke to change the subject.

He'd graduated from a junior college and was exempted from military training because he was the sole provider for his widowed mother. After completing a period of public service instead, he spent the next eight years working at one job, but was kept on a temporary contract and was never offered a permanent position. To me, he was an older, wiser friend who knew the ways of the world. My other friends, who were the same age as me, looked like children chasing mirages, which was probably why he always seemed so much more mature and grown-up. At first, I knew nothing about his family or friends, and I didn't ask. I thought maybe he didn't have any proper friends. I was the same in that regard. The people I knew in the theatre world were all actors and directors; once work was over, we returned to our separate, private lives and only met again on the stage. It was a fantasy world that had little to do with my real life.

Despite having attended a junior college, Black Shirt was no better off than someone who'd only finished high school. Considering that even people with MAs and PhDs were having trouble finding jobs, his lack of steady unemployment was unsurprising.

He started out as a day worker, but lucked out by catching the eye of a field engineer and landed a temporary gig in a construction company. He helped with managing the building materials, construction workers, and the eviction crew, and worked very hard at it. But at the end of each year, he had to sign another contract allowing him to work for another year, all the while being treated differently from the permanent employees. He could not look forward to any paid vacation or educational or welfare benefits, and his pay was only half that of the salaried workers. Naturally, there were no bonuses or incentives either. At company dinners, he had to walk on eggshells and sit there and eat quietly, unable to join the conversation, and he was never welcome at the round of drinks that followed.

He'd never been very talkative, but a few months before it happened, he started growing even quieter. Usually, I chattered away while he listened. Actually, more often than not, he just sat there blankly. And yet I never felt uncomfortable eating or drinking or working with him, because he was so sensible, and because he made no demands of me, and because he never acted like he had to prove himself to me. I felt as free with him as I did when I was by myself. Once, I bumped into colleagues from the theatre while out drinking with him, and introduced him as a cousin. As soon as the words were out, I started to feel like he really was a cousin that I'd grown up with.

*

As rush hour approaches, the convenience store gets busy. There are the customers who come in just for canned coffee, office workers who swig energy tonics and grimace like they're hungover, young people who slurp their ramen cups at the counter against the window, the 'lunch-boxers' who come every single morning to buy pre-packaged meals, women who stop in on their way to work to grab a sandwich and a drink. At exactly 9 a.m., the owner comes to relieve me. Though he had an extra hour of sleep thanks to me, he comes in puffy-faced and looks all around the store. I take off my apron, put on my backpack, and wait quietly in front of the counter. After checking to be sure nothing is amiss, he counts out 60,000 won and hands it to me.

Don't be late tonight.

I'm sorry again about yesterday.

I remember then that today is not only our final rehearsal but also a Friday. After tonight, I am off work for the weekend. At this time of day, all of the buses headed downtown are packed, whereas the buses leaving the city are mostly empty. I doze off the moment I sit down. But my eyes open automatically once my stop is near.

I am walking up the steep road lined with dreary brick rowhouses when I get a text message.

> Heading home? Bet you're exhausted. You said opening night is tomorrow, right? If I can't make it then, I'll go the next day. It's been a while. Miss you.

It's from Minwoo's mother. I pause to send a reply.

> You must have just left for work. I'm almost home. Sooo tired. :(Give me a call when you're able to come, and we'll go out for a drink after the show. :)

I start to head down to my basement room, but pause and go upstairs instead. Studios line each side of the hallways all the way up to the third floor; the fourth floor is where the landlord and his wife live. He is a retired civil servant, and she is always warm and kind to me. I ring the bell. She sticks her head out the door. She knows where I am coming from at that hour. I take out the 300,000 won and hand it to her.

I'm two months behind, right? This is for one month. I'll give you the other month after the show is over.

She clucks her tongue.

It's not healthy for you to live this way, working at night and sleeping during the day … It shows in your face. Are you eating three times a day at least?

Of course. Just trying to make ends meet, you know.

I give her a faint smile and turn to leave, but she calls me back.

Hang on, I have something for you.

She hands me a jar of homemade mustard leaf kimchi from a batch that was sent to her from the countryside. The smell makes my mouth water. I thank the landlord's wife, she asks if I have enough rice to eat with the kimchi, and, our greetings complete, I slowly head back downstairs and stand before the door to my dark, semi-basement room.

5

Choi Seungkwon called me at the office to tell me about a meeting for the Asia World project and a lunch with Chairman Im of Daedong Construction. I wasn't interested, but I couldn't exactly get out of it either, as the opening of the Han River Digital Centre was still a few months away. Besides, while the chairman and Daedong Construction's financial problems and alleged corruption had made the papers more than once, the reality was that the entire construction industry was going through a slump. The Asia World project had been through at least two different project management companies and changes of government administration, and was still not done. Up until I took over the designs for the Han River Digital Centre, Chairman Im had shown no interest in or knowledge of the project. Maybe Seungkwon had finally brought it to his attention. Seungkwon was the younger brother of Choi Seungil, one of my old college friends.

Seungil had majored in art. When I chose architecture

as my major and became more interested in drawing, a classmate told me about the studio where Seungil worked. He was part-timing as an assistant there. The studio had been started by someone who'd graduated from the same school before him; they taught classes to high school students preparing for the college entrance exam. Seungil hailed from one of the civilised, middle-class families of born-and-bred Seoulites. His father was a professor and his mother was a famous designer. I'd gone to his house a few times and was caught off guard to see him and his brothers drinking with their father and smoking freely. But what I envied the most was their study. It was as spacious as the living room and had books going all the way up to the ceiling. Thanks to Seungil, I grew skilled at drawing and sketching. Sadly, he died in an accident right after graduation. He'd always been a lightweight — just one drink would have him nodding off — but for some reason, he overdid it that day, and as he lurched out into the road to hail a cab, he was hit by a bus that was just pulling up to the stop. I found out about it much later from Seungkwon, who said that Seungil's girlfriend had broken up with him that same day. To be honest, at the time, I was busy slaving away as an apprentice at Hyeonsan Architecture for hourly wages, and had missed the news of his death, let alone made it to the funeral.

One year, after I'd returned from studying abroad and was manning a department at Hyeonsan, Seungkwon contacted me. He'd looked me up for business reasons. Even back then he was like a walking encyclopedia, with no end of opinions on architecture, design, and everything in between. He was working for an advertising firm, a subsidiary of a large conglomerate. Later he worked for a foreign ad agency before starting his own company, but he shelved it all once he had made 'enough to live on', to borrow his own explanation. Most of his wealth must've been in real estate.

He'd taken two concepts that had no business being together, culture and management, and combined them to write books and give lectures. It worked, he drew in audiences. The agency he ran, which was some sort of arts and culture foundation with a poetic-sounding name slapped on it, looked just like a playboy social club. I'd gone to his events a couple of times. Everyone feasted, exchanged business cards, listened to talks by the plausibly well-known, and if the mood was right, retreated to one of the members' fancy villas for after-dinner drinks. I was bored of their gentlemanly ways and their talk, oh-so-full of good intentions, but I had to put up with it. Because I knew that everyone there was also anxious and lonely. They all had no choice but to aim for the sunny side of the street. They had to take their tiny, precarious, hard-earned successes and make them stronger and try to grow them. There was little difference between the life I'd lived and Seungkwon's life. The only difference was that I was a bit more cynical.

Sometime last year, I had received a call from Chairman Im inviting me to dinner. When I got to the restaurant, Seungkwon had arrived first and was waiting. We hadn't seen each other in years, but he sounded the same as ever — as if culture was what made the world go 'round.

You're quite the social butterfly. How do you know each other? I asked him.

Im answered, We go to the same church.

This turned into a longer explanation.

He got me and my wife to start attending dawn prayer services.

He said that it wasn't one of the mega-churches but a small church that had been started up by others like him and a pastor that they'd invited. He mentioned a few of the churches attended by powerful political and business figures.

Those places are like social clubs for the upper crust. We, on the other hand, are a purely faith-driven community.

After that, Im had changed the subject to the Asia World project proposal, and Seungkwon gave him the rundown. Based on my experience at Hyeonsan and from starting up my own business, I knew what the deal was. The future of the project would depend on the whims of the current administration. And if it was to be built outside of Seoul, we would have to start with whoever the governor of Gyeonggi Province was and which political party he belonged to. Seungkwon had brought in the proposal and made some connections already, so I figured he would be able to strengthen those connections once the work got started. Guys like him were adept at widening their social networks and forging connections everywhere they went. Standing in the sun was easy. All you had to do was listen closely to what the person with power said, and then say the same thing, but using different words, to indirectly show that you were all on the same page. Sometimes it worked, sometimes it didn't. But even if it didn't, you wouldn't get shoved out to the fringes or anything, because you'd made it crystal clear that your intentions were pure and good, that you were no threat to polite society. It was inane and bourgeois, but the middle classes firmly believed it to be a sound approach.

Hiding my true thoughts was second nature to me by then. I just laughed it all off. And anyway, there was no question that I'd become one of them.

I took the company car to the outskirts of Seoul. At the edge of a broad plain studded with sporadic clusters of apartment complexes stood brand-new buildings of more recent design. In some places, the bare frames of unfinished buildings teetered like steel skeletons, while others had been hastily slapped together with concrete, metal, and glass.

A waiting employee directed me into a meeting room labeled with a sign that read Asia World Preparation Committee. Chairman Im greeted me warmly, while Seungkwon prepared for the briefing. A representative from the provincial office, the director of the Culture Ministry, someone from a financial firm, a bank executive, and a younger man that I didn't recognise were sitting with the chairman.

I know some of you have places you need to be, Im said, so let's get started.

The younger man murmured to Seungkwon, It's true. I have another meeting elsewhere.

Seungkwon turned on the projector and aimed a laser pointer at the screen. The master plan and aerial sketch that had been drawn at my office appeared. He spoke briefly about the Korean Wave. About how K-pop and Korean movies and TV shows were sweeping the rest of Asia and the world, and how there needed to be a centre for the creation of such content. This kind of talk had been going on for years now, but everyone sat quietly through his pitch. His argument was that having a production base alone wasn't enough to sustain creative enterprise, and that if they were to make the best use of the space, there needed to be other facilities, like a shopping mall, a hotel, restaurants, film sets for TV and movie studios, and shared workspaces for musicians and visual and film artists. The ground and basement floors could be used for large-scale recreational facilities, like a spa, as well as outlet stores. He then showed a domed performance arena and theatre. He said that Incheon Airport saw millions of transit passengers every year, and presented a plan for layover sightseeing tours. He mentioned the number of warehouses full of returned and overstock items for everything from apparel to electronics concentrated in western Seoul, and spoke convincingly of the possibilities for a large outlet mall. The blueprints for these plans were both detailed and comprehensive.

The briefing was done in less than an hour, and the first to get up was the younger man. Please send it to me in writing, he said and left. Later, Seungkwon told me that it hadn't been easy to get him to come and hinted that he was from the Office of the President. He invited me to the lunch that followed, but I told him I had another meeting as well and stood to go. As a matter of fact, I'd made plans to go to the opening of Kim Kiyoung's retrospective. The whole way back, I felt like I was exiting a tunnel from another world. It was all a dream, wasn't it? While you chased your dreams, the truth emerged only to turn into another dream and vanish. The steel and cement structures pockmarking the land looked different to me now, like it was all just a virtual world inside of a video game.

*

At the entrance to the retrospective, I ran into Youngbin and a couple of architects. Most of the visitors were students and people well known in the architecture and cultural industries. Some of them had known Kiyoung personally, but many hadn't known him at all. The exhibits featured his sketches, drawings, and designs; one room housed his models, and another had photos and videos. One of the videos showed him talking.

Korean architecture during the colonial era was a re-copy of the pseudo-modernity that Japan had copied from Europe. This is evident in the Seoul Capitol building and Seoul Station. Immediately after the war, with money and materials in short supply, makeshift structures were erected on top of the gruesome ruins of the city. These lasted barely a decade before needing to be rebuilt. Houses built for the working class and hillside shantytowns created countless new roads and alleyways. When conditions began to improve, traditional architecture was reinterpreted, and the traditional colours of wooden architecture were applied to concrete instead. This was the work of the generation before us, whereas our generation poured its energy into redevelopment of slums and the creation of concrete mountains covered in boxlike apartments. But we paid a heavy price for it. We drove our neighbours into a space of distorted desire. Architecture is not the destruction of memory, it is the delicate restructuring of people's lives on top of a sketch of those memories. We have already failed horribly at achieving that dream.

The interview cut to a scene from a documentary of a small project that Kiyong had worked on in a remote mountain town in the countryside. It showed him sitting on the porch of a country house, holding the hand of an elderly woman. What are you building? she asks. A township office, he answers. Don't build that, she says, that's useless for us. Then what would you like me to build? he asks. Build us a bathhouse. We sweat all day in the fields, and the women have nowhere to wash up, and the old folk have nowhere to soak their tired bones. Okay, he says, I'll build it for you. Can I trust you? she asks. Of course, of course. The screen fills with their hands: his long, slender architect's fingers that have never lifted anything heavier than a pencil clasping her hand as gnarled as dried wood.

Kiyoung was resting in the gallery office. Friends were visiting with him in pairs after taking in the exhibit. I sat next to him.

Thank you for your help, he said.

I never realised just how much you've done.

I meant it, too. His accomplishments were modest compared to the colourful changes the city had undergone in the past decades. My colleagues and I had been naïve enough to talk derisively about him behind his back. But though he had mostly designed smaller buildings in small towns and provincial cities and remote parts of the country, they were novel for being public buildings. In photos, they looked quaint.

Youngbin asked me, You haven't seen his work in person, have you?

I didn't answer.

Of course he hasn't, said Kiyoung, his voice frail and wheezy. He's a busy man. When would he find the time?

I did happen to see your experimental clay house project on Jeju Island, I said.

Ah, that was cancelled. As is everything that's not profitable enough.

We had nothing else to say after that. I stared vacantly at the other people who kept butting in. Everyone knew he didn't have much time left, so they were sparing with their words. When he switched to his wheelchair to return to the hospital, everyone scattered, as if they'd been waiting for his cue.

Youngbin invited me out for a drink, but I lied and said I had to be somewhere. When I got home, I poured myself a glass of whiskey and, on a whim, dialled Soona's number. I don't know why I did it. I guess I just felt lonely. It hits me sometimes, this loneliness, like when I wake up with an aching stomach after a night of heavy drinking, or when I'm eating alone, or while doing the laundry, and again when I'm hanging wet laundry on the rack to dry, and once, when I was sick with the flu for a week. It just hits me, like a wave of hunger. But when I called, a recording said, 'The number you are calling is no longer in service. Please check the number and dial again.'

Kiyoung spent the rest of the retrospective confined to his bed, and in mid-August, when the summer heat wave was at its peak, he passed away. Now he was just handfuls of ash sitting in an urn. This gave everyone another excuse to gather and drink to excess, get rowdy, catch up on the past, and part ways again.

I'd forgotten all about my phone conversation with Soona last spring, the same day I'd gone on that outing to Ganghwa Island to see Kiyoung. I couldn't help wondering if I'd just imagined that phone call. Already, the ginkgo trees outside my townhouse were changing colour.

I got an email notification on my phone, but these old eyes of mine couldn't possibly read such tiny text. I turned on my laptop instead. I didn't recognise the email address, but I knew it was meant for me because the first line said 'Dear Mr Park.'

A lot has changed since we last spoke. Due to some unforeseen circumstances, I won't be accessible via phone.

My mind was a mess after we talked. Memories from the past that I'd long forgotten all came back to me, as vivid as if it were yesterday. No, I take that back. I never forgot them. I've never forgotten a single moment from my life. After my husband passed away and I was raising my son on my own, I used every bit of free time I had to write down everything that ever happened. I guess you could call it a diary, or my memoirs. I know it's silly to fancy myself a writer, but it was a way to alternately comfort and chide myself. And to remind myself that I've had a good life.

A few months ago, I'd lost my one and only son and had lost all hope when, suddenly, there you were. It was so strange. I found out by accident that you were giving a lecture right downtown. I don't know why I didn't go to it. I'm disappointed in myself, but also a little relieved. You looked so old in your photo. Which is why it's good I didn't go. You didn't see what I look like now, so instead you can remember me as pretty Soona, forever in her twenties.

It's difficult for me to explain exactly why I decided to write to you like this. I guess I just wanted to talk about everything that has happened to me over the years, like telling an old story to someone you've been friends with forever. Though I don't resent the thought of how quickly the years of my life have flown by, I do hope you'll humour my desire to complain about it to someone who knows me well. I hope that my sharing what I've written with you won't leave you feeling put out or, worse, like I'm asking for something from you. The memories of checking out library books with you and talking about great works of literature are still fresh and new. Those days I spent with you are precious memories for me now, and I can only hope that I was just as memorable to someone else. Is that greedy of me? If you don't want to read the attached file, just delete it. I won't mind.

I opened the file. As I pictured her sitting at the computer, typing her life story one word at a time, an astonished smile spread across my face. Just as she said, I kept picturing her as a twenty-year-old, not as she would be now. I simply could not imagine her in her sixties. She'd said she didn't go to the lecture because she was embarrassed at being fat; I assumed she'd filled out like all women her age do. A lot of people say they regret reconnecting with their first loves, but considering what I'd done, I was in no position to be disappointed. Moon Hollow was long gone, like a memory of some taxidermied thing. And once something is gone, it does not return.

My father was fifteen years older than my mother. He was thirty-five when he evacuated to Busan alone during the war, my mother barely twenty. Actually, I say that like he was an ordinary refugee, but in fact he'd been conscripted into the Communist army and then taken prisoner and held in a POW camp on Geoje Island. Maybe he had good connections, because he said he ended up being grouped with the anticommunist POWs and released. One day, he showed up at my mother's parents' noodle house on Yeongdo Island, still dressed in his threadbare uniform, and asked for a job. The factory was originally Japanese-owned, but after Liberation, the owner had gone back to Japan, transferring all of the rights to the shop to my grandfather.

My mother and I were both noodle-house daughters. I had an uncle, three years older than my mum, but he was dragged off during the war and never returned. I've only seen him in photos. With my uncle missing, my grandfather was probably relieved to have my father show up on his doorstep right when he was in need of a worker. He never did take down the little sign that read 'Moriyama Noodle Shop.' It's there in all of our old photos. As refugee shacks cropped up all over Busan, my grandfather cranked out noodles night and day but could still barely keep up with demand. After finishing middle school, my mum had to stay home to help with the work, and two more employees were hired in addition to my father. I used to wonder how my thirty-five-year-old father landed my twenty-year-old mother; to use a common expression, maybe he was a national hero in his past life, and she was his reward. My dad was very straight-laced, not much of a talker, the type who could focus solely on a task at hand until it was done. This would have earned him my grandfather's full confidence. He was completely different from my grandfather. My grandfather left the running of the shop to my father and began spending time away from home; this naturally brought my mother and father closer together. Though my mum also said that her mother nudged her towards him. The shop was doing so well that my grandfather bought up the houses on either side, and then the house behind ours as well. He started drinking all the time and hanging out in hostess bars, and moved into his own place. He had a child, a boy, by another woman, after which he stopped coming home at all. When my grandfather abruptly sold off the shop and the houses, my father headed blindly to Seoul, with my mother and grandmother in tow. I was in the third grade at the time. Making noodles was the only skill my father had acquired after coming to the South, but it worked in his favour. They used the money that my grandmother had managed to hold onto, along with a loan, to purchase a used noodle machine. They didn't have enough money to open a shop in a large marketplace in one of the nicer neighbourhoods, so they went instead to a slum neighbourhood on the outskirts of the city. That was Moon Hollow.

Up until I started high school, I was the only girl in that whole neighbourhood who was attending school. I liked to read, and my grades were pretty good. There was one boy who also went to high school. Like me, he was the only male student from our neighbourhood. I don't remember exactly when he moved there.

Everyday I would come home from school, grab a book, and head straight to the attic, where the noodles were hung to dry. I would hole up in there for the rest of the day. It was my own little world, a place where I could escape reality. My grandmother passed away a few years after we moved to Seoul, but our livelihood stayed the same. We weren't rich or poor. My father made just enough to support the three of us.

It's a little embarrassing to admit this, but I knew that the boys in my neighbourhood liked me. They would pretend they were fetching water from the tap just so they could hang out next to our wall, four or five of them at a time, making all kinds of noise. Most of the time it was Jaemyung and his brothers and the shoeshine boys. I also remember that the kid they called Tomak used to follow me around and pester me all the time. But I never saw Park Minwoo with them. He was different. I thought the other boys were all bums, and it shamed me to know that I lived in the same place as them.

Our neighbourhood was so poor that only a few houses had glass windows. Most windows were covered with boards that let in no light or air at all. I still remember how excited I was to get a glass window installed in my bedroom for the first time. It was a day in spring, and I'd just started middle school. My room had always been dark and stuffy, even in the middle of the day, and I couldn't look outside unless I removed the boards. But after my dad installed a glass pane, I could lie in bed and fall asleep to the sight of the night sky bursting with stars, and the warm sunlight that dazzled my eyes in the daytime felt like a blessing. On rainy days and snowy days, I could be found glued to the window, gazing outside.

I was standing in the window the same day that Park Minwoo, the fishcake house son, appeared on the road below, walking toward our house with something in his hands. He stopped for a moment and seemed to hesitate. I stepped away from the window so he wouldn't see me watching him. My heart raced for no reason, and I blushed. After a moment, I heard him call out, asking if anyone was home. He'd brought us a package of leftover fishcake; to this day, it is still the tastiest fishcake I've ever had.

After that he came over often to buy noodles or to bring us fishcake, and we saw each other all the time at the bus stop or on the bus. The first time we met outside of our neighbourhood, it rained. He didn't bring an umbrella, so he shared mine for the three blocks to the library. He offered to carry the umbrella, his hand brushing mine, and I hurriedly pulled my hand out of the way. But his clothes ended up drenched all the same, *as he insisted on keeping most of the umbrella over me.*

At the North Seoul Library, I checked out Herman Hesse's Knulp *and he checked out* The Brothers Karamazov. *Then I waited for the due date, when he and I would see each other again. On the way back from the library, we stopped at a snack bar, where we ate steamed buns and sweet red bean porridge and talked about the books we'd read. To my surprise, he brought up the subject of our bleak, uncertain futures. I think maybe he felt anxious about hanging out with a girl when he was supposed to be studying for the college entrance exam. I had good grades and was still a year away from worrying about the test, so I was more or less relaxed. He kept repeating the fact that he wanted to get out of Moon Hollow. And that the only way out was through studying.*

Getting coal briquettes into our neighbourhood in the winters was a huge hassle. The briquette vendor refused to deliver them, saying that the steep hills made it too dangerous. Each time it snowed, the roads turned to ice, and all of the families would come out to transport their own briquettes, strung two or three at a time on short pieces of rope. My father ended up dying of carbon monoxide poisoning because of those briquettes. At least one or two people got sick and died from it every winter. I got a little sick once as well, when I was in elementary school. My mother told me to drink some kimchi brine, but I pretended to be on the verge of death and badgered her to buy me a digestive tonic called Gasmyungsoo. Back then, I was hooked on carbonated drinks, like Coke, Sprite, and Fanta, and the sharp fizziness of Gasmyungsoo in particular was so good that I would feign stomachaches just to get a bottle. One morning, I woke up needing to pee, and on the way back from the bathroom, I spotted a bottle of another health tonic, Bacchus, sitting on a windowsill in the milky light of dawn. I immediately grabbed it and swigged the whole thing. I felt something oily slide down my throat. I thought I was going to throw up, but I suppressed the urge and went back to sleep. Later, I was woken by the sound of my grandmother grumbling over the mysterious disappearance of the camellia oil she used on her hair. I stuck my face over the chamber pot and vomited it all up.

At some point as I grew older, I started thinking of Moon Hollow as a snug, cozy place to live. Every family had so many kids that the alleyways were filled with the sound of raucous laughter day and night. And even when they'd screamed bloody murder at each other all night long, their frenzied voices carrying through the walls, you would still see couples being tender with each other in the morning: wives with swollen faces handing packed lunches to husbands leaving for work. Sometimes I'm overcome with longing for the sight of *women gathering at the tap to do laundry and fetch water. When it rained, everyone stayed in their narrow rooms, and the neighbourhood grew quiet. With the sound of raindrops sliding down the roof and dripping from the eaves, a sweet sleepiness would wash over me.*

I remember the first time he took my hand. We'd decided to go further from home for a change, and ended up heading all the way downtown to the Gwanghwamun district to watch Love Story. *I still remember the snowball fight between Oliver and Jenny. I cried my eyes out when she died of leukemia. That's when he took my hand. With one hand in his, I used my other hand to wipe the tears from my cheeks.*

And how could I forget the excitement that gripped not only our fellow merchants in the marketplace but the entire neighbourhood of Moon Hollow when he found out that, after turning in his application and fretting for weeks, he'd been accepted to the best university in Korea? It was a banner day for us all. That winter, the whole world seemed to belong to Park Minwoo. And since it was winter vacation, he and I were able to see each other several times a week.

Then I, too, started my third year of high school. With Minwoo away at university, I saw less and less of him. We fell out of contact. At one point, I risked the embarrassment of calling on his parents to buy fishcake and ask when Minwoo was coming back. They told me he came home once every few months, but only to wolf down a quick lunch after which he always headed straight back to school. They added that he was working as a live-in tutor for a wealthy family and earning his own tuition. That inspired me to study hard, to try to do as well as he had. I gritted my teeth and buckled down, knowing I only had to endure one more year before I could get out of Moon Hollow, too.

Her story ended there abruptly. What was Soona trying to tell me? Why the long-winded life story? And what was it leading up to? Questions followed upon questions, and faint memories started coming back to me. Just as she'd remembered, after starting college, I became like a traveler or a tourist to Moon Hollow, dropping in only occasionally, and naturally didn't make it back at all while doing my army service. After I got out of the army and returned to school, I was busy applying for jobs and, after graduation, I was working my tail off at Hyeonsan and barely made it home once or twice a year. Around the time I left to study abroad, my family was finally able to buy a house and get out of Moon Hollow. But my father passed away soon after the move. In the years that followed, slums all over the city were earmarked for urban renewal, and our old neighbours were scattered far and wide.

At any rate, I was lucky enough to get into a top-tier university and set myself on a new path. After getting out of the slum, my eyes were opened to so many new things. Most of our neighbours had been from Jeolla Province, whereas Soona's family and mine were from the rival Gyeongsang Province. We were like black beans that had accidentally sprouted in the middle of a soybean patch. I'd thought that we were all the same in our poverty, but after leaving that tiny world, I learned that being from Gyeongsang, the southeastern province, meant something very different. The generals and politicians who'd seized power and ran the country were all from Gyeongsang, and even most businessmen and industrialists were from there as well, which meant that I could walk into any company or government office and feel immediately at home thanks to my accent. It even occurred to me that I would have had a much easier time of it if I'd stayed behind in Yeongsan, rather than going to Seoul with my parents, and finished high school nearby in Daegu instead. Had I done that, I would have built a wider network, and reduced my hardships by at least half. I would have been surrounded by people who'd gone to the same schools as me, or were related to me by marriage, or had grown up near me.

No sooner did I start college than President Park Chung-hee's Yushin dictatorship began. Everything was in turmoil, and not a day went by without riots and school closures. My classmates were being arrested left and right, and every time I went to class, there were fewer and fewer of them. I was determined not to go back to Moon Hollow. I was like a mule in blinders: I went back and forth between the library and the classroom in silence, and did not consider any other path. In my spare hours, I tutored students on the college entrance exam, and ended my days by going back to my rented room near the school and collapsing from exhaustion.

I shared the room with someone who'd come from another part of the country than me. It was uncomfortable having to live with a stranger, and even harder to have to cook together and eat at the same table. What made matters worse was that he was a wannabe activist. At least, that's how I thought of him. He should have gone into the factories to help organise 'the people' or gone down to the countryside to bond with the farmers, but instead all he did was smuggle pamphlets and banned books and lead a little study group in our room. Because of him, I was forced to give up on the idea of living independently, and became a live-in tutor instead, but that turned out to be a lucky break. My father's status as a former clerk in a township office won me the rare opportunity to be around a whole new class of people.

It's not that I was already cynical at that age or anything. I sympathised with those who were fighting social injustices, but at the same time, by having the fortitude to just buckle down and get through it, I was able to forgive myself for not getting involved. Over time, this turned into a kind of habitual resignation, and it became second nature for me to regard everything around me with an air of cool indifference. I thought this meant I was mature. During the 1980s, when most people were finally getting a breather from the grinding poverty of before, this type of resignation became commonplace, and all of those small wounds calloused over. It was like having a corn on your toe: it pains you constantly, and you swear up and down that you've got to remove it, but at some point, it ends up simply being a part of you. And only now and then are you vaguely aware of that foreign intruder inside your sock.

6

I open the door with its many locks and am met with a familiar smell. Actually, it's a mix of smells, but the strongest is the smell of mould, which seems limed with cold air. The building was built on a spot excavated out of a hillside; except for the front, the rest of the building is practically underground. My one small, rectangular window that just barely peeks aboveground is covered with metal bars, and the only view it offers is of the legs of people walking up and down the alley. The worst part is that the back wall isn't properly waterproofed; the humidity in summer and the temperature difference between inside and outside in the winter mean that the back wall is constantly damp, and the mould has taken deep root there. It worsened after my room flooded during last year's rainy season. Kim Minwoo had warned me that living in a place like this would make me sick, and he'd brought over a container of waterproofing liquid, which he sprayed all over the wall, then applied a layer of thin styrofoam and a fresh sheet of wallpaper for me. But the mould just came creeping back over the winter. This summer, the rains were much lighter, but the mould still left its ferocious marks. I would soak a cloth in bleach and wipe the wall clean, only to have it come right back. As I lie in bed, looking up at that stain spreading across the wall, I suddenly feel breathless, like I am suffocating, and fight the urge to scream hysterically. But at least now the air is dry, so it will be liveable for the next few months. I look around at my room anew. One mattress, a sink, a gas stovetop, a microwave, a small refrigerator, a washing machine inside the dark utility closet, a cheap desk and chair, a wardrobe, and two pale fluorescent lights, one in the middle of the room and one over the sink. That's everything. It's a well-equipped room for a single tenant. My landlord doesn't complain much even when I'm a month or two behind in rent, because he knows that tenants like me aren't easy to find, and I, too, am in no position to demand much of my landlord. So I do not complain.

I lie on my old mattress for a while, but I'm not sleepy. I get up and sit at the computer instead. I've been struggling with insomnia for the last few months and haven't been eating properly, and now, my hair has started falling out, and the loose strands all over my room annoy me. How long has it been since I last came home from the graveyard shift at the convenience store and collapsed from exhaustion directly into a deep sleep?

Lately, other than my shifts at the store, I've been

staying locked up at home, surfing the internet in a daze, or else scribbling things down at random. After our last play ended, I considered submitting something to a screenplay contest. But it was hard to think in terms of camera angles after having written for the stage for so long.

There's so much information available online that I don't have to leave my room to know what's happening in the world. Whenever I feel stuck on a piece of writing, I download a movie to watch or play a game online. Writing, games, theatre — it's all a virtual world to me. As for the new game I've been playing lately, I don't know exactly how to explain it, but it's quite creative. And a lot more fun than online solitaire. Anyway, this one is a two-player game, so I have to stay alert to avoid making any mistakes.

I open a file labelled 'Foxtails' that I created recently and slowly re-read what I've written so far. The cursor blinks over the last sentence. It was a sloppy way to end it, but I'd had a terrible headache at the time and was unable to keep going. I hit return and start to type, 'I didn't know it at the time, but something terrible was lying in wait for me', but then pause to give it careful thought. If this were my own story, could I bring myself to tell it? Something is off. This next part won't be easy to write.

I check my email. I delete some spam and then check the status of the email I sent a few days earlier. It says it has been read. But still no response. Not that I know what I am waiting for anyway.

Next, I skim the news. Times have been tough; there are more stories of gruesome murders lately. Most turn out to be over money. I read an article on construction and, as has become my habit, type the name Park Minwoo into a search window. A long list of articles about him come up. I notice an old article that says he's taken on the Han River Digital Centre project. Articles, blogs, websites, photos, videos, tweets — there's more information here than any one person could need. But can any of this really sum up who he is? I bought a copy of his book recently. *The Architecture of Emptiness and Fullness.* It cost 15,000 won. That's a lot for someone who only makes 60,000 a day. I could have checked it out from the library. Considering that I avoid buying any books that aren't strictly necessary and try to borrow them from the library instead, buying that book made me feel like I was haemorrhaging money. But I'm glad I bought it. It's not limited to just architecture, but touches on a lot of different subjects. He covered some of it in the lecture I went to, but seeing his actual writing makes it easier to see what kind of architect he is, what he thinks about, what his philosophy is.

I'd wanted to draw a connection between him and Kim Minwoo, seeing as how they shared the same name. But when I jumped to that conclusion, Kim Minwoo's mother laughed at me like I was pathetic. That's the best your imagination can come up with? she'd said. You better start writing soap operas instead of plays. I turn my eyes back to the computer screen, close the browser and open another file on the desktop. 'Black Shirt.'

*

Last summer, my semi-basement room flooded. I couldn't bring myself to go inside. I called him, and he rushed over in his jeep. Without a word, the two of us went to work bailing the muddy water out of my room and kitchen. Everything was damp, including all of my bedding, so I had to spend a few days away. I got an air mattress and camped out at the theatre, which was also in the basement. When Minwoo saw my setup, he suggested I stay at his mum's place instead. So I decided to go ahead and impose on her for a few days. It was kind of funny to stay at a man's mother's house when we weren't even married, but I had no other option.

His mother lived in Bucheon, between Seoul and Incheon. She had a small, 14-pyeong apartment with one small room and a combination kitchen-slash-living room. She wasn't home when we arrived. Minwoo boiled up some ramen and set the table with a side of kimchi. We were up on the twelfth floor; a cool breeze wafted through. It was far more liveable than my little semi-basement room. A long bookshelf that looked out of place sat against the wall that led from the front door to the kitchen and living room. I was surprised to see it so stuffed with books. There were some I'd read, and some I'd been wanting to read.

Are these all yours, Minwoo? You must read a lot.

My mum likes books … Luckily, I take after her.

He turned on the vacuum cleaner, and I helped out by giving the kitchen sink and bathroom a quick scrub. His mum didn't get home until after 11 p.m. I found out later that she worked at a big retail store in downtown Bucheon. She was pretty and girlish; I would not have guessed that she was in her early sixties. Her roundish figure was the only thing that really gave away her age. She seemed happy that I was visiting, and immediately went back out to buy beer and snacks from the nearest convenience store, then set to work peeling fruit. The three of us sat around an old-fashioned, aluminium tray table.

Her room flooded, Minwoo said, asking permission for me to stay. It'll only be a few days.

His mother readily agreed.

You and I hardly see each other anymore these days, she said. It'll be nice to have someone in the house.

She did not pry as to where I worked, where my family lived, or what our relationship was. The only thing she did ask was how old I was. When I told her I was twenty-eight, she said it was a good age to be. She said that twenty-eight means you're old enough to be mature and know something of how tough life can be, while still being young and full of energy.

Not her, Minwoo interjected. She knows nothing about life. She quit her job to go into theatre.

His mother studied my face and nodded.

That's a brave choice. So you're getting by while doing plays?

Minwoo glanced up at the clock and stood.

I better get going, he said.

Already? You're never here, and already you're leaving? We have a guest.

I have a job that starts early tomorrow. Woohee will be here the whole time. That's okay, right?

Of course.

After he left to return to his goshiwon in the city, his mother and I finished the last of the beer and stayed up talking until after midnight.

When she asked me out of the blue, Aren't you ever getting married?, I took it in stride. Lately, all of the older people in my life had been asking me that same thing. I just chuckled.

My generation has given up on that, I said.

All you have to do is love someone, she said. It doesn't matter if you're rich or poor. Everyone acts like everything is fine, but on the inside, we're all lonely. It's always the same for people like us. Nothing gets any better, and nothing ever changes.

But you don't seem like someone who has suffered, I said. You look young and pretty, like a wealthy lady.

She laughed hard at that.

Thanks for saying that, she said. I did get a lot of

compliments when I was your age.

I stayed for four days. Meanwhile, Minwoo called up a friend of his and fixed the drain in my apartment and even redid the wallpaper in my room. Though his mum wasn't much of a talker, she was always cheerful and friendly. When I told her I wrote plays, she seemed to open up to me more, because she started telling me all kinds of stories. She told me that she'd once got an essay published in her high school magazine, and that Minwoo's father was a bookworm as well. He'd died young, after being injured in an accident. They'd had Minwoo at a relatively old age for the time. She'd had a daughter before she met Minwoo's father, but she'd lost that child to measles. She told me the area used to be all peach orchards, and that in the spring, when the peach blossoms were in full bloom, there were more honeybees than flies.

The day I was getting ready to leave, she suddenly said, I wish you lived here with me.

Thank you, I said. I'll come over often.

*

One day, Minwoo asked me, Why theatre?

It took me a while to answer. I wasn't used to being asked that so bluntly and was caught off guard.

Well, I guess, because it's what I like to do …

You want to do theatre, but it doesn't pay the bills,

which is why you work so hard at your part-time job. I get that. But then, what am *I* working for?

Isn't it the same for both of us? We both have things we'd rather do, but none of it adds up to a livelihood?

Minwoo spoke slowly, stumbling over his words as he often did.

No, we're not the same. I'm not like you. I don't have ambitions. I think I'm just doing one thing after another, at random, trying to convince myself that there really are people like me in this world. Everyone else lives for today while gauging what will happen tomorrow, but I've spent nearly a decade constantly on the move, my feet barely touching the ground. Each year, I signed another contract, worrying about what would happen if I didn't, while all around me, the guys I worked with kept disappearing. And eventually, I was laid off, too.

He talked about how male bees, or drones, get kicked out of the hive in autumn. He said you could find them clinging to walls or trees in the chilly mornings, as still as if they were dead, but at midday, when the autumn sunlight finally warmed up, they would stagger off to fly among the wilted chrysanthemums. They were expelled from the hive by worker bees to avoid wasting food on them, and the no longer useful drones, with nowhere to go, would wander for a day or two before dropping dead on the frost-covered ground. Then he talked about a Western he'd watched. Settlers raced on horseback toward the horizon and stuck flags into the earth to claim acres and acres of land. Could you imagine, he said, what would happen if all of Korea did that? If everyone gathered on Jeju Island or along the southern coast and raced each other to claim their homes, individual flags raised high? He said he would probably do no better than to race like mad for his mother's apartment and lie in the tiny room shared by mother and son, exhaling in relief.

Minwoo's last assignment before he was fired from the construction company was to assist a section chief at a demolition site. Everyone there, from the other contract workers like him, to the regular employees, to the hired muscle sent from an eviction service company, knew how the project had come to be. The construction company had its fingers in everything — the consulting office, the city planning committee, the municipal council, the district office, and more — and had nominated the head of the development committee and its members in order to push the project through at lightning speed. The slum residents were forced to leave because they couldn't afford the new apartments that were being built. Some had already been pushed out of several other neighbourhoods that had gentrified, and they had nowhere left to go. Most said they'd lived in ten different places before barely managing to set down roots there. They made clumsy protest banners and stood in rows — women, children, and the elderly — to shout at the eviction company's hired muscle, but gave up after only a few minutes in the face of those terrifying men charging at them with hammers, metal pipes, and bulldozers.

In the past, when slum neighbourhoods were rebuilt, construction company employees would go door to door to offer some form of appeasement and get their signatures, but nowadays the process went no further than a reconstruction committee's approval. The construction companies warned their workers to refrain from violence and avoid any physical contact in order to limit bloodshed, but later, that too ended up as little more than a formality, a way to assign blame. Burly men yanked and shoved, cursed and ridiculed, tore women's clothes, slapped people's faces, and knocked them down. Perfectly good buildings were ruthlessly demolished, the excavators letting out their terrible roars, while helpless shouts and cries rang out from among the protesters. The families would hold out for three or four days, but as the streets filled with wreckage and rubble, they would start to leave, one or two at a time, and the community would fall apart, as splintered and fragmented as their demolished homes.

While the demolition was taking place, Minwoo moved into one of the abandoned houses with the men from the eviction service company so they could keep an eye on the site. After the neighbourhood was reduced to rubble and looked as if a bomb had been dropped squarely on it, a line of dump trucks came in to clear away the wreckage, and the once sprawling neighbourhood returned to its original form as a small, shabby, fallow plot amid the towering buildings of the city. During his month on-site, Minwoo naturally became friends with the men he bunked with. He grew especially close with one guy in particular, the leader of the eviction crew, a scrappy type who spat out a curse between every other word. Minwoo's friend had a rap sheet for assault. The eviction service company provided both demolition experts and so-called security guards, the latter of which were known for being well-built and good fighters. They were routinely deployed not only to demolition sites but also to labour strikes. One day, while the two of them were drinking, Minwoo's friend asked him to guess what his dream in life was.

Minwoo said, You're telling me you still have a dream? Now that's something.

I had this cellmate in prison. He was kind of a pretty boy, like a gigolo? I thought maybe he'd sung or played guitar at a hostess bar or some place like that. He was always drawing something after lights out. I grabbed it from him once to see what it was. It looked like a blueprint. He said it was the racetrack in Gwacheon.

Your cellmate's dream was to strike it rich at the tracks?

You could say that. He was planning to rob it.

After he got out, he never saw the musician again. But he couldn't forget the guy's plan and went down to the racetrack to have a look around. There were a dozen ticket booths, each of which collected tens of billions of won every weekend. Each booth was staffed by a female ticket taker and a security guard, and the door was equipped with an electronic lock. The code to the lock was changed every time someone entered and would automatically shut down in an emergency. It'd be an easy job if you could get one of the ticket takers in on it, he said. He added that you would need at least four accomplices.

Sounds to me like you've watched too many movies, Minwoo said.

The guy said nothing in response, but showed him several mobile phone photos he'd taken of the racetrack. Minwoo bunked with the guy and his big dream for a month.

One day, the excavator operator alerted Minwoo to a problem. One of the families was still holding out in a house at the very top of the hill, making it difficult to clear the area around it. Minwoo took some of the eviction crew with him and ran up the hill. The excavator had already taken down the courtyard wall and was stopped in the yard with the engine running. An elderly man was lying on the ground in front of the excavator, and a middle-aged man who looked like his son was holding a two-by-four. Two women and three children stood nearby. One of the children, a tall, skinny boy who looked like he was in his teens, shouted something and kept twisting his body this way and that. The crew leader gave his usual instructions.

What're you standing around for? There are only four adults. Pull them out of there!

The goon squad were used to this sort of thing and went in slowly. They were in no rush. They reasoned with the family, each of them saying things like, Just calm down, and, You wouldn't want to get hurt now, and, There's no point in fighting anymore, it's all over. They dragged the adults away one at a time. The women and the elderly man were dragged out kicking and screaming, but the middle-aged man, who appeared to be the head of the family, swung the two-by-four and refused to leave. The crew leader who'd bunked with Minwoo caught the two-by-four with his hand, twisted it out of the man's grasp, and tossed it away. The children cried as they followed the adults out, but the skinny teenager let out an awful shriek and ran towards the excavator that was just that moment swinging around like a giant hand. Before anyone could shout a warning or stop him, the boy ran head-first into the metal arm of the machine as it turned. The boy's frail body flew into the air, as limp as wet laundry on a line, then slammed down onto the ground. Too late, the engine shut off, and the operator stepped down. He took one look at the bloodied boy lying on the crushed cement and yelled into the faces of the crew.

You all saw that, right?! He ran straight into me!

One of the women who'd been muscled off the lot wailed and ran back to throw herself over the boy.

The crew leader said to Minwoo, Rotten luck. Better call an ambulance.

Minwoo called an ambulance and contacted the head office. The family, now covered in the boy's blood, raved at them. The boy had died on the spot; they said he was intellectually disabled. Reporters swarmed, and construction was put on pause. Minwoo returned to the head office and spent nearly a month on standby before being let go. He never saw his friend, the crew leader, again. The racetrack in Gwacheon bustled with crowds every weekend, but nothing ever happened.

7

The thing about memory is that two people can end up with different versions of the same event. Either the storyline gets distorted because of your emotional state at the time, or you inadvertently forget that it happened once time has moved on. That was the case for Soona and me. She made it sound like I'd waltzed off to college and all too easily forgot her and Moon Hollow, but it wasn't quite like that.

I pored over Soona's letter again and thought about my first trip home after starting college. I'd been stuck either at school or in my rented room the whole time and wasn't able to get away until the semester ended. I spent several afternoons at my parents' shop, frying fishcakes so my father could take a break. One of the employees had quit after burning her hand on the deep fryer, and the shop was understaffed. Summer was always a slow season for us anyway, so my father had decided to wait until the weather cooled off to hire someone new. Between the hot, sticky weather of the rainy season and having to stand in front of a vat of boiling oil, I was drenched in sweat front and back. Adding to my misery was the sheer physical exertion of kneading ground fish into the soy and starch dough. It only took me a few days to understand, to feel in my very bones, just how hard my father, with his lame leg, had been labouring for years.

I think it made my parents uncomfortable to accept my help. My mother was busy bragging about having a son in college to all of the other vendors, but once evening rolled around and the shop began to get busy, my father would silently shove me away from the deep fryer.

One day, I wrapped up the leftover fishcake with the torn edges and headed to the noodle house, just as I had in the past. When I opened the door, Soona's mother greeted me.

Oh, my! Look at how grown up you are now! I wouldn't have recognised you on the street.

She made such a fuss that Soona's father came out too, followed by Soona poking her head around a door. But Soona's face looked haggard, and her expression was dark. She gave me a curt nod and disappeared back into the room.

I grew up without any sisters, and coeducation still wasn't much of a thing at the time, so I knew nothing about girls. I was completely taken aback; I had no idea why Soona was being so cold to me. At the same time,

I felt embarrassed to realise that I'd let myself get distracted by a pretty girl and squandered precious studying time on her, and I dealt with the disappointment by reminding myself that I had to snap out of it if I was ever going to make something of my life.

After Soona's house, I stopped by Jaemyung's shoeshine at Hyundae Theatre. By then, the brothers had built the business up and acquired a small, seven-pyeong workspace on the first floor of a building in the alley. They'd gone from working under a tent on a street corner to having an actual shop. The shop was divided into an office space for Jaemyung, with a desk and chair, and a workspace where the boys could clean shoes, complete with a row of folding chairs and stools. The chairs were for customers who came in person to have their shoes shined, so they could sit and leaf through newspapers or magazines as they waited, while the shoes that had been fetched from off-site customers were lined up in order to one side. Jaemyung managed around ten shoeshine boys, while Jjaekkan oversaw eight. Now that they had a proper base right in the entrance of the market, they no longer had to worry about guarding their turf near the theatre and coffeeshop and could wander freely all over the neighbourhood, collecting shoes for shining.

That was where I finally heard the rest of the story of the taekwondo master. Everything had been quiet for a while after Jaesup knocked the guy out. But then the master sent

Tomak to challenge Jaemyung to an official match. His conditions were that they would fight in the elementary school playground across the street at six in the evening, but only the actual fighters, the teacher and Jaemyung, could come, along with one observer each. Jaesup had vanished after beating up the master; he had a criminal record and had never been the type to stay home for very long anyway. Tomak probably figured that without Jaesup around, Jaemyung would be no match for him. What Tomak and his master didn't know was that Jaemyung had more martial arts training than his brother and was far more skilled at actual street fighting. But they did know his weakness: he was responsible for keeping his family fed and sheltered and could not leave the neighbourhood. He was in no position to start any trouble. They figured the master's mistake was in meddling with Jaesup, an ex-con and a runaway who fought dirty and flew by the seat of his pants. When Jjaekkan and Jaemyung saw me, their faces lit up and they told me the whole story, acting out the fight scenes as they went.

It was last May, right? Jjaekkan said. He closed up his taekwondo studio so fast, he must've bet both his livelihood and his reputation on beating us in that fight.

At 6 p.m. that day, the only people on the playground were a few kids kicking a ball and a couple of elementary school students dragging an adult-sized bike around and falling off it as they tried to learn how to ride. Jaemyung and Jjaekkan met Tomak and his master, who were waiting for them in front of the school gate. Let's go somewhere else, the master said, too many eyes on us here. Jaemyung suggested the back of the school. It was blocked off by a wall and had a sizable yard that would later be turned into a parking lot.

The master was dressed in a taekwondo uniform and a windbreaker. Jaemyung was in a cheap business suit. He was a boss now, after all. The master took off his windbreaker and handed it to Tomak, loudly cracked his neck to the left and right, jumped around to warm up his muscles, and tightened the knot on the front of his belt. Jaemyung took off his suit jacket and handed it to Jjaekkan, then unbuttoned the top two buttons of his dress shirt. They both got into a fighting stance and started circling each other. The master came in first with a roundhouse kick. Jaemyung dodged it and, in a flash, grabbed the master by the collar and flipped him. The master struggled to get up as Jaemyung rained a flurry of punches down on his face. *Biff, pow, bam*, and he was knocked out again. The taekwondo master never even had the chance to put any of his taekwondo moves to use.

It was over in less than five seconds! Jjaekkan said.

Jaemyung had turned to Tomak, who was standing there looking stunned, and said, That's the guy you trust to have your back? Better watch yourself from now on.

Jjaekkan crowed about how he didn't believe in belts,

and how only those who'd been in actual street fights were unbeatable, as if he'd won the fight himself instead of Jaemyung.

Jaemyung was convinced that the master had only challenged him to a fight because he was already planning to skip town. Maybe the guy thought that he'd use his skills to break Jaemyung's arms and legs and then close up shop. But in the end, it became even harder for him to find students willing to learn taekwondo from him, and he had to leave town anyway with his tail between his legs.

Tomak was not so easily daunted. Whenever he bumped into Jaemyung, he would greet him halfheartedly and quickly make himself scarce, but whenever he ran into Jjaekkan, he'd say, Tell that brother of yours he better watch his back.

After the fight, Jaemyung told Jaekkan to start giving a little money now and then to Tomak and his friends. When Jjaekkan protested, saying that it was beneath him and that Tomak didn't deserve it, Jaemyung explained, Kids like him are just hungry. It's like the saying, give an extra rice cake to your enemy. It pays to be kind.

But then, right before the start of summer vacation, Tomak went and committed an unforgivable sin.

Jaemyung took me to a small shop nearby and bought two bottles of beer. He'd been acting a little differently towards me, speaking a little more politely. It wasn't just that, now that I was in college, he was acknowledging that

I was no longer a child. He seemed awed by the fact that I had ascended one step into a world that he and the others couldn't enter.

You know who Tomak is, right? he asked. I'm so pissed at him. I have to teach that piece of shit a lesson. He drank his bottle of beer in one long swig. Listen up. A few days ago, Tomak grabbed Soona as she was coming home from school. He was lying in wait for her.

He told me that several people, as well as Jjaekkan's shoeshine boys, had seen her running toward the public tap, panicked and crying, the shirt of her school uniform torn and the skirt covered in mud.

Almost all of the kids in our neighbourhood envied Soona for being the only girl there to go to school, but no one knew that she and I had been close. We ignored each other at home, took separate buses whenever we hung out, and on our way back, deliberately kept our distance from each other once we were near the entrance to the market. It tore me up inside to hear Jaemyung's story. He'd heard from a kid who knew Tomak that Tomak had been so bold as to follow Soona several times and wait for her in front of the school. Jaemyung had sent some of his boys to bring the kid to him. But instead of giving him an earful, he'd taken the kid to Manseok Grill House, right across from where he worked, and plied the kid with bulgogi and soju to get him to talk.

And now I'm going to teach Tomak a lesson. You in?

I finally began to understand why Soona had avoided me earlier when I showed up at her house with fishcakes, why she looked so sombre, and why she had ignored me the few times we'd bumped into each other on the street before that. I was fuming and wanted to beat Tomak to a pulp. On top of which, it hurt my pride to see Jaemyung just as angry and stepping up to do something about it, as if it were his responsibility.

Jjaekkan tried to hand something to Jaemyung. It seemed he'd already prepared a stash of implements to fight with.

Keep it, Jaemyung said. I'm good with my fists.

I saw a few of the smaller kids huddled together, Jjaekkan said. Let's go bash their heads in with these.

Jjaekkan kept a bat for himself and handed me a two-by-four. We headed towards the shack where Tomak and his gang hung out, the shoeshine boys leading the way across the main street and up the hill. We took a left at the dead-end street and followed the path down and around to the back of the hill. It was the northwestern slope, facing away from the rest of Seoul, so the neighbourhood there was even poorer than ours. The shack was in the second alleyway. We stood in front of the door for a moment and listened to the loud laughter coming from inside.

Jaemyung pressed his ear to the door and then whispered to us, Tomak's in there. I'll go in and bust them up. You guys wait out here and beat up anyone who tries to escape.

He kicked in the flimsy plank door and rushed in. The lights went out, something smashed through the window, and we heard shouting and fighting. One boy came flying out the door. Jjaekkan and I swung our weapons in the dark, not caring whether we hit his head, his back, or his limbs. As he sprawled on the ground, another boy came running out, and we went after him, too. After we'd picked off four boys that way, like smoking badgers out of a den, Jaemyung stuck his head out of the door.

Come on in. It's over.

Jjaekkan excitedly asked where Tomak was.

Flat on his back in here, half dead.

Jjaekkan and I went inside. Jaemyung turned on the kitchen light. Tomak was bloodied and spread-eagled on the floor. The room was covered in broken glass from the shattered fluorescent bulb, soju bottles, and glasses, and clothes were strewn everywhere. Jaemyung nudged Tomak in the ribs with his foot.

Hey, quit faking it and get up.

Jaemyung sat him up. Tomak slowly stirred and wiped his bloody mouth with both hands. Jaemyung barely managed to suppress his anger long enough to deliver a stern lecture. It struck me then that he, more than any of the rest of us, really did look like Soona's man.

If you show your face around here again, you're dead. We haven't told the adults yet what you did, you little shit. If her parents press charges, you'll go straight to prison. So you're going to leave first thing tomorrow and never come back. Your father is too old and works too hard at that factory to see your arse behind bars. Understand me?

Jaemyung took out his wallet, pulled out some cash, and tossed it on the floor in front of Tomak.

There's your bus fare.

*

That autumn, I started my job as the live-in tutor to a high school sophomore and escaped my miserable rented room. I'd inherited the job from an older friend who was going into the army. As he led me along the residential street lined with mansions tucked behind high walls, I could feel myself start to shrink.

I met the student's mother in a living room with a two-storey-high vaulted ceiling. My friend had told me with a sigh that he'd been tutoring him ever since the boy had started high school, but his grades and class ranking hadn't gone up enough yet. He lacked focus and could never seem to carry what he'd learned over to the next day's exam.

The boy's father was an army general. If I remember right, he had two stars and was an infantry division commander. He had one son and a much younger daughter. The officers and enlisted men who came and went from time to time would all stand at attention and salute the general's wife.

I had my own bedroom there, which looked out on a

hill thickly wooded with deciduous and evergreen trees, but while teaching or doing my own studying, I was allowed to use the general's library. Between all of the teaching and studying I did, I put Moon Hollow out of my mind completely. When the general's wife asked where I was from, I told her Yeongsan.

As for my student, I'd wanted to be both a trustworthy big brother to him, and a friend to whom he could open up. He was only two years younger than me, but he was as immature as a middle school student. That was probably due to his being an only son who'd been spoiled his whole life. Nevertheless, he was so uncomfortable around his father, the general, that he could barely get a word out. When the tutoring began, he flat out ignored me and sat there with a contraband Playboy magazine spread open on his desk instead of his textbook. I let it go at first.

After a month of that, I took him with me to Moon Hollow. Noting the reproachful looks from my parents, I left him sitting in the store while I took over at the fryer for an hour to give my dad a break. After that, we went to Jaemyung's shoeshine. Jaemyung took a break from working to buy me some alcohol. He poured a glass for my student as well.

I could tell that Jaemyung's mannerisms and style of talking made the kid nervous. His usual bravado was gone, and he was red-faced and short of breath after just a few shots of alcohol. Clever Jaemyung started to exaggerate.

You have no idea what a big deal Park Minwoo is around these parts, do you? Anyone who doesn't know his name is bound to get their skull bashed in. And to think that he just up and decided one day to turn his life around, and then got into one of the best colleges. I swear! It's weird to picture that hand of his holding a pen instead.

The kid tried hard to hide his surprise that I was from a slum and was friends with thugs. I hadn't taken him there to try to scare or intimidate him. I just thought that if I showed him my true self first, then he would open up to me. Regardless of how he took it, I wanted him to realise just how privileged and advantaged he was compared to me. I don't know if he ever got that, but the visit to the slum paid off, even if the day didn't go quite the way I'd planned.

We decided to keep the trip a secret. If his parents found out that I'd taken him out drinking when I was supposed to be making him study, he and I would have both been in a world of hurt. He told me what he really wanted to do with his life. He said he wanted to become a movie director and travel around the world. To put it another way, he meant that he hated studying and wanted to spend his life playing. I told him it was a great idea and gave him this really cliched speech about how making his dreams come true would take some work, and that the only way he'd be able to do whatever he wanted was to first get his grades up. I used the idea of studying abroad as bait. I told him to work hard at his English so he could qualify for studying abroad, after which he could travel, study cinema, and gain experience to become an international film director. I suggested that we go hiking or camping once a month in exchange for studying hard the rest of the time. It would give him a chance to get away from home and school, and us time to develop our relationship as mentor and student.

I guess he really did come to think of me as a big brother, because he started telling me about things that happened at school, and even his grades gradually improved. During exam periods, he stayed up with me, studying late into the night. When his grades reached a certain level, I had a discussion with his mother about his future. She was shocked to hear that he wanted to become a movie director, and said that the general would never allow it. I told her that they had to respect their child's opinion if they expected him to feel motivated to do anything for his own future, and I convinced her that film studies had many other practical uses besides directing. I tutored the boy until his third year of high school, when he was accepted to university. That was how I laid the first stepping stone towards my own career.

After finishing my third year of college, I decided to fulfill my army service. The general retired from active duty and, following Chun Doo-hwan's coup d'etat, rounded out his career as chairman of a state-run firm. I benefitted greatly from the general's largesse, starting with being able to complete my military service without leaving Seoul, and also studying abroad after graduation. He has since passed away, but his wife is still as healthy as ever and living with their son.

The general's son and I ended up becoming like brothers. He went to work at a TV station after college and now runs his own production company. I can't really take any of the credit for how well his life has gone, but I definitely benefitted from knowing his family. What I learned from him was that being born with a silver spoon in your mouth meant you could do pretty much whatever you wanted. As long as you weren't a complete fuck-up, your life would stay more or less on track. For me, escaping the poverty of that terrible hillside slum and living a completely different life was a miracle in and of itself — you can't help but get a little more complicated on the inside when that happens. People like me need something to soothe the discord. I mean, truth be told, most people are like me. I see them whenever I look out the top-floor window of a hotel lounge in the heart of the city, down at the high-rise apartment buildings, red neon church crosses, and streets filled with the light of shops and restaurants. During the days of dictatorship held together by oppression and violence, we must have sought comfort in those churches, in owning the luxuries sold in those department stores. Or maybe we fell back on the media's constant deluge of 'justice through strength'. We needed the props and people that we'd made together to pacify us endlessly, to tell us that we'd made the right choice in the end. I, too, was just one small piece of the machine, just another cog that had narrowly managed to find comfort in their midst.

*

From the time I started working as a live-in tutor up until I left to study abroad, I saw Soona several more times and still remember each of those occasions clearly. That's because each one corresponded with a change in my life. One day I got a call from her at the general's house. The housekeeper told me there was a call for me, and I assumed it was my mother. We didn't talk on the phone very often, but whenever something important came up, she made a point of calling. I said hello, but there was no response. Then, after a moment, I heard her quiet voice say, This is Soona. She told me that she'd gotten my number from my mother and was at a café nearby. When I found her, she seemed out of place, almost scandalous, in that ritzy neighbourhood. Her outfit looked sloppy, and she was sitting in the corner facing the wall, restlessly fussing with a cheap vinyl bag that she'd stuck on the seat next to her.

Where are you going? I asked.

I left home, she said without hesitation. Before I could say anything to that, she continued: I heard you're going into the army.

I had heard that she didn't get accepted to any colleges on her second try, so I tried to ask indirectly whether she was going to try for a third time.

How've you been? I asked. How's the test prep going?

I'm giving up on college. My dad told me to get a job.

Is that why you left home?

I was so much in the habit of being a live-in tutor that I couldn't help slipping into a teacherly voice. Soona let out an abrupt, unnatural-sounding laugh.

What'm I, a kid? We're barely a year apart.

I was just worried …

She asked me to buy her a drink. She seemed like she'd been waiting for this moment. She even threatened me, saying that she wanted to spend time with me and might just up and die if I refused her. I got nervous. I couldn't decide what to do. Maybe it was the anxiety of knowing that, even though I thought I'd escaped the slum, Soona had been there all along, ready to drag me right back. I still wanted her, but I was in a different place emotionally, and had used my tutoring job as an excuse to avoid her and put distance between us. It might have also been the discomfort of having crossed over into a new world only to be suddenly confronted with your old, familiar world. Or, to put it more precisely, while watching Jaemyung take the initiative to punish Tomak for his evil deeds, I'd felt like my own precious emotions had been sullied. I didn't want to take any further part in the ridiculous shenanigans of slum kids.

And yet, there was Soona, who'd sought me out and was sending me all kinds of signals. I'd be lying if I said I hadn't thought about her every minute of every day since the first time we met in Moon Hollow. I pictured her body every time I masturbated. My selfishness took her by the hand and escorted her to a bar. Well before the government-imposed midnight curfew — when all citizens were supposed to be indoors, and which young couples would conveniently break as an excuse to spend the night together — we went straight from a drink at the bar to a motel, and that night I was clumsy but passionate.

The next day, under the bright glare of the sun, she told me she'd see me when I got out of the army, the cheer in her voice sounding forced. The street was filled with people, buses, and cars as everyone was heading off to work. For some reason it all looked strange and unfamiliar. I frowned, as if from the sunlight, shaded my eyes with my hand and said,

I'll drop by sometime.

*

And then the years passed. I finished my army service, went home to see my parents, and bumped into Soona at the corner of the market. Well, I didn't exactly bump into her. She was walking home from the bus stop, and I was coming down the pedestrian overpass when I spotted her. I'd been back before that but had deliberately avoided looking her up. She didn't see me. Soon she was walking away from me, the distance between us growing. I hesitated for a moment and then called out to her.

Cha Soona ...

If she hadn't heard my quiet voice, I don't think I would have called her name a second time. She somehow managed to hear me, though, and turned at once.

Oh, it's you!

We both glanced around. Hometown Coffeeshop had been replaced by one of the western-fusion restaurants that were trendy at the time. The kind of place with partitions between the tables for privacy and plastic clusters of grapes or fake ivy leaves as decoration. Soona was wearing a simple dress, and her lightly made-up face was as pretty as ever.

When did you get out of the army?

About a month ago.

What about college?

I'm planning to go back. Where are you coming from?

Work.

I thought you were leaving the city?

I got a job at a small company in Seoul.

What do you do there?

Bookkeeping and stuff. No big deal.

Still, that's good. It's not easy to find a job these days.

It wasn't that hard, actually. My father knows the owner.

So you've got connections.

It was a predictable conversation, the standard niceties between two people who'd grown up in the same neighbourhood.

Then, as if in passing, I asked,

No marriage plans?

Without a moment's hesitation, she said, Maybe when you graduate … She giggled and added, I hope that doesn't scare you.

There was nothing more to say after that. We sat in awkward silence for a moment, and then she murmured, Be right back, and left her seat. I leisurely smoked a cigarette and waited for her to return from the restroom. Twenty minutes went by. Bewildered, I got up and went to the counter. I checked the bathroom and the entrance, then went to settle the bill, when the waiter said,

The lady paid right before she left.

*

I went home to Moon Hollow a few more times before finishing college, but never went any further than my parents' house. Right before graduation, I had my interview at Hyeonsan Architecture and began working there. It had been recommended to me by my advisor. I started out as a trainee. Back then, the work was endless, and I slept almost every night curled up on a couch in the office. I was on a team with other trainees, including Lee

Youngbin. But even in the midst of that crushing workload, during my second year there, I found the time to apply for a government-sponsored study abroad program, and I passed. That was the same year that all that trouble happened in Gwangju. The country was in turmoil. We were under martial law. Tanks were parked on city streets, and special forces soldiers in full camouflage and carrying bayonets stood guard outside TV and radio stations, government offices, and school gates. Rumours were quietly spreading of a civilian massacre in Gwangju.

I'd never been to Gwangju in my life, but after hearing the whispers of older colleagues, who in turn had heard whisperings from others, the fact that I had no connections to Gwangju didn't put my mind at ease. We all had a pretty good idea of how the previous president had died the year before, and we knew exactly what sort of ambitions the new military-led regime held. But regardless, what we were constantly weighing was whether and how the prevailing political winds would affect our own plans. We took the crumbs that those in power tossed our way and used them to grow our own wealth. And even if we did privately feel some guilt about it, we all knew the feeling wouldn't last. In fact, we still know it. Later, upon arriving in the US, I saw the foreign press footage and photographs of Gwangju and was shocked to the core. A sense of powerlessness plagued me for a long time after.

Right after finishing my army service, I'd gone back

to my job as a live-in tutor and stayed there up until I was settled in my own career. The general's daughter was one year away from starting middle school, so I tutored her in English. My room on the second floor, including my furniture and books, was exactly as I had left it. They treated me like I was the eldest son. They'd worried about their son growing up lonely, since he didn't have any brothers of his own, but they saw how completely he trusted me and relied on me. I ended up being his mentor, even though I was hardly able to take care of myself.

After starting work at the architecture firm and deciding to study abroad, the general's wife started dropping hints about what other future plans I might have. She told me that one of her friends had a lot of daughters, and that the youngest daughter was smart and pretty. Her siblings were all studying abroad already, and she, too, was set to leave once she finished school. So the daughter and I met, as arranged by the general's wife, and soon an offer of marriage was on the table. I was honest with her and her family about my background. Her father had travelled the world as a diplomat, which may have been why he was so lenient about our poverty. He implied that all that mattered was that I was smart and talented.

It had been a long time since I last saw Soona, when she ditched me at the restaurant in Moon Hollow. I'd been back a few times since starting work. Of course, I never asked my mum about her or went back to the noodle house. It wasn't deliberate. I just felt like Soona had no place in my life anymore. Sure, I'd slept with her right before going into the army. But so what?

And then, one day, I got a call from her at the office. My heart no longer raced as it used to, and there were no more butterflies in my stomach. Instead, a sense of guilt slowly crept over me. What had she been doing with herself all that time? I realised that I hadn't thought about her at all.

I met her in a coffeeshop downtown after work. She was wearing a men's windbreaker that looked like it was part of a work uniform; it took me a moment to even recognise her. Naturally, I took her to dinner, seeing as how she was an old friend and someone from my hometown. Storm clouds brewed in her face. I asked how she'd been and learned that her father had passed away while I was in the army. I'd had no idea that they'd lost the noodle business. She didn't seem particularly bothered by the fact that I knew none of this. I asked if she was still living in the same house. She told me she'd moved, but only to the neighbouring village, and was still more or less living in Moon Hollow. I asked if she was still working at the same place, and she told me she'd quit recently. We didn't part ways immediately after dinner but instead went to a pub and ordered draft beers. I got drunk, but not plastered.

How did you find out where I work? I asked.

She looked at me with a straight face and said, Why? Did you think you could run away from me? I can find out anything I want about you anytime I want.

Then she giggled, as if she was messing with me just like old times, but her smile vanished as quickly as it had appeared.

I hear you're leaving the country? she said.

It was stupid of me to ask how she knew. Her mother and my mother saw each other all the time at the market and would of course have shared such news with each other. And besides, the first thing I'd done after finding out that I passed the exam for studying abroad was to go home and tell my parents and then treat Jaemyung to a celebratory drink. By then, Jaemyung had moved on from the shoeshine business and had opened a bar. It was the kind of upscale establishment where clients were treated to young female hostesses who sat beside them to keep them entertained. The booths were partitioned to form private rooms, and there was even a live musician. Jaemyung had a head for business and knew the area like the back of his hand; it would have been strange if the business didn't do well. That was probably when I told Jaemyung that I was getting married.

Soona and I had a lot to drink that night. As the midnight curfew drew near, I started getting ready to leave.

Actually, she said, I have a favour to ask.

The whole time we'd been drinking, I'd had a feeling that there was something on her mind.

Do you have any connections in the military? she asked. Someone high up?

… What's wrong?

Someone I know was taken away.

Anyone I know?

She nodded. All at once, I realised who it was.

It's Jaemyung, isn't it?

She lowered her head. I'd thought the windbreaker looked familiar.

Were you two … living together?

No, not together. But he's been looking after my mum and me.

She explained that a few days earlier, the local police chief and a detective had picked Jaemyung up at his bar, and no one had heard from him since. She'd gone to the station with Jaemyung's sister, Myosoon, to ask what happened, but no one would tell them anything; all they could get were rumours that he'd been arrested and taken to a military camp. A nationwide order to round up gangsters had been issued. Well after the round-up was complete, they found out that Jaemyung had been placed in the Samcheong Re-education Camp.

I walked her out to the curb and hailed a cab. Before getting in, she threw her arm around my neck and hugged me.

Goodbye, she said. Congratulations on getting married.

I stood there long after her taxi had left.

*

Though I wasn't crazy about it, I couldn't bring myself to do nothing at all about Jaemyung. After a few days of dilly-dallying, I carefully brought the subject up with the general. He listened and then asked who Jaemyung was to me. I told him Jaemyung was a distant relative, and that he wasn't a gangster, just the owner of an adult entertainment establishment. Without getting up from the sofa, he picked up the phone and called someone. He read off the name and address that I'd jotted down on a scrap of paper and told the person to take care of it. That was all it took.

After that, I officially proposed to the girl the general's wife had introduced me to, and left for America with her. Around the time I completed my studies, her father, the retired diplomat, passed away. The rest of her family emigrated to the US, and we held our wedding in New York. My parents were unable to attend, so we had a simple wedding attended only by her family and the friends we'd made in America.

8

Up until it happened that winter, I didn't see Kim Minwoo for nearly a month. His mother texted me once to invite me over, but I never found the time. I managed to get my play staged, but it didn't do well, which left me feeling depressed and apathetic about everything. My boss hurriedly ended the run and switched back to rehearsing a foreign play. It was a long, depressing winter, with hardly any fun and nothing to hope for. Minwoo hadn't called me either, but I was so busy trying to get by that I felt no desire to try to check in on him. When I think about it now, we didn't have that heat that you'd expect between a man and a woman. I felt relaxed and reassured whenever I was around him, but my feelings for him went no further than that.

Then, on one of those frigid mornings when the snow has fallen and the clouds have cleared away, leaving behind a crisp blue sky, I got the phone call. I'd turned off the sound, so my cell phone was vibrating and wiggling around on the table. I didn't recognise the number. I decided not to answer it, but then a text message arrived, asking me to contact an Officer So-and-so at some police station. I hadn't done anything wrong, but I knew that when it came to any sort of bureaucracy, it was best to be compliant. I called back immediately. Is this Ms. Jung Woohee? Yes, what is it? Ah, I'll have to explain in person. I asked if it was urgent. It was obvious to me that he was holding something back. For a moment all I heard was breathing. Then he said, If you're at home, I can come to you. It was my turn to pause and catch my breath. He said it would take only five minutes and asked me to send him my address. I said okay. The police station must not have been very far, because my doorbell rang in less than thirty minutes. I already had my coat on. I didn't want to let him in my apartment. I opened the door to find a uniformed officer standing there. He spoke before I could even step foot outside.

Do you know a Kim Minwoo?

Yes, I do.

He's committed suicide. I would appreciate it if you would accompany me to the station.

I was stunned, like I'd been hit over the head.

What? What did you just say to me?

Kim Minwoo is dead.

At the station, the officer wrote my statement down line by line in a notebook: 'We were just friends. We were not dating. I met him while working at a part-time job and came to think of him as my brother. I have not seen him in a month.'

I asked if they'd contacted Minwoo's mother, and the officer said, How do you think we got your number? There were two phone numbers written down in his suicide note. His mother's and yours. So, you never observed anything unusual?

I said that Minwoo had always been outgoing and hard-working, that he was cheerful and driven, and was holding down three different part-time jobs. Then it was my turn to ask questions. The officer told me that his estimated time of death was five days ago, but that he'd been found only that morning, next to a river in Chungju, about two hours southeast of Seoul. His beat-up Galloper jeep was parked next to an Avante. It was winter, the road unpaved and far from the highway, so not many people passed through. The local residents said that some people did go there sometimes to fish and had thought nothing more of it. But then a day passed, and another day, and then three and four days, and still those two cars were there. Wondering why two unknown cars had been abandoned for nearly a week, they called it in, and the police contacted a tow truck driver. The driver arrived and checked the inside of both cars only to discover people dead inside. There were four in the Galloper — two in front and two in back — and two more in the Avante. The

edges of the windows, the vents, and even the gap around
the bottom of the steering wheel column had been sealed
with duct tape. Soju bottles and plastic cups littered the
floor, and a portable camp stove was covered in charcoal
ash. Minwoo was in the driver's seat of the Galloper. Next
to him was a man believed to be from Ansan. In the back
seat were a brother and sister from Chuncheon. The man
and woman in the Avante had different addresses — Icheon
and Chungju — but based on their ages, their clothing,
and the photos and videos on each of their cellphones, it
was conjectured that they'd had a common law marriage.
The six of them had probably met on a suicide pact website
or a social networking site. There was no way of knowing
who the ringleader was, but it was clear that Minwoo and
the man from Icheon, the two car owners, had picked the
others up and brought them there. According to phone
records, they'd all started talking to each other several
months earlier and had met regularly in person. There was
even a photo of several of them drinking beer and eating
fried chicken at some pub on the outskirts of Seoul.

What must it have been like to meet people with the
goal of dying together? I wondered what he'd written in
his suicide note. But why … I mumbled, half to myself. As
if there were any point in asking. After all, I, too, had once
thought how nice it would be to die as quietly and easily
as falling asleep in my room. To just fall asleep and not
wake up. But it never went beyond a thought. As soon as I

opened my eyes, a day passed, and then another. Everyday life in its tenacious continuity.

The body was delivered to his mother after a perfunctory autopsy. As with most families of suicides, she opted to skip the usual funeral arrangements and go straight to the cremation.

I dialled his mother's phone number and said, It's Woohee. Her voice sounded sunken. Wicked boy, she said, and was quiet for a long moment before asking if I wanted to join her. She gave me directions to the city-run crematory north of Seoul, at the foot of a hill, way out in a remote part of Gyeonggi Province. To one side was a memorial park and the columbarium where the ashes were housed; in front of me was a marble-panelled building that looked like a hospital. I found Minwoo's mother right away in the waiting room. I had learned from the police and now from the bereavement register that her name was Cha Soona. She was holding a number and waiting for her son's turn. There were at least ten incinerators; an electronic screen in the waiting room listed the names and numbers of those currently being cremated. I sat next to her and held her hand. When his number came up on the screen, we were guided over to where we could observe the cremation. I saw flames rise behind the fireproof glass. His mother didn't cry, but just stared silently into the fire.

After a while, we were guided over to where his ashes were collected. A worker poured them through a kind of net to catch what remained of his bones, and then those, too, were ground into a fine ash. We took Minwoo's remains in their small clay vessel and went to the area that was designated for scattering ashes. Lingering patches of snow speckled the surrounding hills, and frozen clumps of earth crunched beneath our feet with every step. The entire process took barely more than an hour. Minwoo's mother wrapped her knitted scarf around the lower half of her face and invited me to her apartment.

The whole way there, in the taxi and on the subway, we were each quietly lost in our own thoughts. She stopped by a local market to buy fruit, boiled pork, blood sausage, fishcakes, and two bottles of soju. When we got to her apartment, it was exactly the same as before, except chillier somehow. On a small, shabby folding table, she set out the food she'd bought and slowly poured the soju into a nickel kettle.

I can't exactly hold an ancestral rite for my own child, she said, so I figured I would offer a silent prayer for him to be reborn in paradise.

She said this in an offhand way and tried to smile at me.

I don't have any photos of him that would work as a funeral portrait either, she added, so let's just pretend he's standing over there in front of the window.

She poured some of the soju into a glass and spoke to the empty air near the window.

Drink up. I brought you that blood sausage you like, too.

She lowered her head and closed her eyes. I prayed silently with her. When I raised my head, hers was still down, and tears were falling from her face and onto the table. I held my breath and stayed quietly at her side, watching as her tears pooled. She took out a tissue and wiped her face and blew her nose. Then she let out a long sigh, as if shaking it all off, and looked up.

Okay, now it's our turn to have a drink.

I picked up the kettle and poured her a cup of soju, then poured myself one. We downed it in one gulp and immediately drank several more shots. She opened the backpack that had been found in Minwoo's car and rummaged through the clothing, mobile phone, and miscellaneous items, and then handed me his suicide note. It was written on a piece of paper ripped out of a notebook. On the front was the letter and on the back were her address and phone number and my mobile number. I took the letter in a daze and stared blankly at it.

Dear Mum,

I'm sorry I couldn't take care of you for the rest of your life. You'll find my laptop at my place in Seoul. Please make sure you get it. I worked like a dog to be able to buy that.

It's not much, but I transferred my savings into your account. Please use that money to go to the doctor for a check-up. Make sure you go! And take Woohee

with you. I think she might be really sick. She really
needs to move out of that basement room … Please tell
her that I'm sorry I couldn't help her.
Mum, I love you.

At last, the tears came. Stupid Minwoo, worrying about everyone else when he was the one dying. It must not have felt real to me yet at the crematory, I'd felt embarrassed at my own lack of tears. But now, here I was, a burst dam. Minwoo's letter, which he must have scribbled down while sitting in the car, made me remember that slow voice of his, the way he always tried to sound so business-like. I kept drinking.

His mother asked, Did you love Minwoo?

I didn't answer. She looked at me for a moment, then her voice turned melancholy.

You should have loved him.

9

The chairman of Daedong Construction was arrested for embezzlement and malpractice. I'd heard about the arrest a few days earlier from Choi Seungkwon, but I didn't know the exact charges until I saw it on the news. While selling lots in the Han River Digital Centre and pushing ahead with a new project, he had taken out a substantial loan using a company he'd recently acquired as collateral, which caused heavy damage to Daedong. Then, he invented fake tenants and used corporate funds to purchase apartments and Digital Centre commercial lots in order to make it look like the units were selling better than they were. All that, just to expand the business more aggressively and fundraise for Asia World. I think I know what he was praying to God for at those dawn prayer services. And hadn't I, too, hoped earnestly for his prayers to come true?

When I got to the office, Song whispered to me, You have a visitor.

A visitor? What's it about …?

He opened the door to my reception room without a word. Two men, one in a suit and one in a windbreaker, set down their coffee cups and stood up hesitantly.

We apologise for dropping in on you like this.

The man in the suit handed me a business card: they were police investigators. I stopped Song as he was turning to leave.

You better sit down, too, I said.

The two investigators looked me straight in the eye and asked how I had become involved in the designs for Daedong's Han River Digital Centre. They asked if the plans for Asia World had been drawn up by us as well. I felt annoyed, but I didn't let it show.

All we do is draw pictures at the request of building owners. I assume you're not here to buy blueprints from us?

The man in the windbreaker said, According to our investigation, Asia World is a complete scam. It's just a front for raising capital.

I decided to ignore that and asked, Is this a formal investigation?

No, of course not. The man in the suit waved his hands. It's just that there's been a lot of talk lately, and we're looking for some help. If the Asia World plans were drawn up here, then we'll need to see any and all paperwork.

I turned to Song and asked, Do we have anything like that?

The plans and promotional photos should already be online.

I stood to go into my office, but before closing the door all the way, I said, I've got work to do, so I'm afraid you'll have to excuse me.

Song saw the two men out and came to see me again.

I gave them a little something for their trouble.

Song said it like it was nothing. He was an old hand at this. I blushed. I spent the rest of the morning feeling antsy. I kept thinking about how Youngbin had once told me to drop everything. I went to Google Maps and sat there looking at various plots of land, studying the shapes of the mountains and coastlines. It struck me suddenly that maybe I wasn't looking for the future site of the house where I would spend my waning years, maybe I was looking for my future resting place. The thought calmed me. There was not much time, no new people, and no new work left before me. I did have five new emails, though. I opened the one with 'Foxtails' in the subject line. Just as I'd thought, it was from Soona. As with the last email, there was a brief message and an attached file. This time, she addressed me by my first name instead of 'Mr Park.' It gave me a warm, fuzzy feeling.

Dear Minwoo,
It was spring when I first saw you in the news, but already the lush green leaves are changing colour,

and the chilly air at dusk has me buttoning my coat higher. I can't help but think that if we were to measure our ages in seasons, then this would be us. The days of our youth are probably now nothing but photographs in some treasured album, yellowing and fading like memories over time. And yet, my memories of you are still so clear, and lately they grow more vivid as the days pass.

Please know that I'm not asking for anything from you. I'm simply relishing old memories as one does at this age. After losing my son, I thought that I was all alone in the world. I felt scared and frightened. But then you appeared. Like I said, please don't feel pressured by that. These are my thoughts alone. I feel like I've seen an older brother who was lost to me when I was young, and nothing more. I am not asking for or expecting anything from you.

As long as I can share these old stories with you over email now and then, I'll be happy with that. But if you don't want these emails, then this will be the last I ever send you. I just want to tell you about the things that happened to me after you left, just to get it all off of my chest. I think that might be the only way that I, too, will finally manage to escape Moon Hollow. Actually, I take that back. You were the one who wanted to escape. I ... honestly, miss the place.

I opened the attached file. Soona said she missed Moon Hollow, but it sounded like she was still stuck there. Her story drew me in, like she was leading me by the hand, back to Moon Hollow. When I read the part about my showing up there after a long time away, right around the time Tomak attacked her, I could tell that she resented me for not having been there for her. She said that after that happened, she locked herself in the attic with a stack of books. And, of course, the one who comforted her and helped her was Jaemyung. Whenever there was a good movie in town, he got free tickets for her from the boy who put up the movie posters, and whenever they needed an extra hand in the noodle house, he rolled up his sleeves and dove right in.

I knew that once Minwoo escaped Moon Hollow he would never come back. And honestly, when I thought about what an awful sight I was, I didn't want him to ever see me again. I knew that he dropped by sometimes to visit his parents, but I stayed hidden for fear of bumping into him. Luckily, he never looked for me.

Jaemyung found various excuses to drop by our house during my year or so of hiding. I knew from rumours that he had stepped up and beat the hell out of Tomak, and that Tomak had disappeared from our neighbourhood ever since. My parents treated Jaemyung like a son. How could someone like me ever be good enough for a man like Minwoo? I realised that no one knew me better than or understood me and cared for me as much as Jaemyung did.

I heard that Minwoo was going into the army. I decided to accept Jaemyung's love, in order to free myself of my feelings for Minwoo. But as the date approached for our planned visit to Jaemyung's hometown, where we would visit his father's grave, I found myself despairing over the fact that I was going to grow old with him there, in Moon Hollow, and I wanted nothing more than to run away. I don't know what I was thinking when I went to see Minwoo. He sounded more disconcerted than happy on the phone. I was already feeling waves of regret, but I couldn't turn back. I felt like I just had to see him once, no matter what. I was so flustered when we met. I asked him to buy me alcohol. I should have got up and left then. But I figured I'd already messed things up as badly as I could, so they couldn't get any worse. I chose to think of it as my personal way of sending him off. The next morning, when we parted ways on the sidewalk, I forgot to get on the bus and ended up walking for several bus stops. Other people kept glancing at me crying as I walked. I muttered out loud to myself, Goodbye, Park Minwoo, you and I are through. That was his send-off.

After my father died, we closed the noodle factory.

Running the machine to knead the dough and extrude the noodles was too much for my mother to handle on her own.

Jaemyung was pretty much my husband by then, just without the wedding ceremony. With his help, we bought a house across the street, on the corner of the entrance to Moon Hollow, and opened a small store. I quit my job to help my mom out at the store. Jaemyung came by once every few days and spent the night with me. He was the one who told me that Minwoo was leaving to study abroad with his fiancee. Then, a few months or so later, Jaemyung was arrested. Rumours went around that each police station had a quota to fill, and so a lot of people I knew got rounded up. I couldn't bear the thought of having to see Minwoo again, but I had nowhere else to turn.

A month later, Jaemyung came home. He was all skin and bones and looked exhausted. It took over a year for him to recover. I moved in with him to help nurse him back to health, and soon after we had a little girl. But he never was able to return to his old cheerful and outgoing self. His stint in the Samcheong Re-education Camp didn't just ruin his body, it destroyed his spirit. He swore at first that he was going to keep his distance from bars and the like, but once he was on his feet again, he started hanging out away from home and meeting his old crew. I didn't find out until much later, but he opened a gambling den and even started doing drugs. We used to call these illegal gambling dens 'houses'. They made money by hiring professional gamblers to fleece big spenders of all their money. Jaemyung bought a used foreign car and showered me with jewelry, and I believed him at first when he said that he'd made the money by selling alcohol wholesale. But after just a couple of years of this, someone was killed in a gang fight, and Jaemyung was rounded up again. He was sentenced to fifteen years for being part of a crime ring.

Not long after he went to prison, our little girl died of measles. I didn't tell him, but he must have heard it from someone anyway. I went to visit him one day, and he refused to see me. The guard handed me a note from him that read, 'Stop visiting. We have no child now, so find your own way to make a living.' Then he applied to be transferred to another prison. I tried visiting him there, but he always refused to see me.

I moved back home with my mother. She'd been lonely working in the store by herself. I was there all of three or four months when a man came to our store. He was so awkward and hesitant. He was selling books on monthly installment plans door-to-door. He was shy, nice, and about three years younger than me. He told me that being a book peddler wasn't exactly a suitable career, but he'd tried all sorts of odd jobs after graduating high school and had barely managed *to secure that position. I loved reading, and was drawn to a thirty-volume collection of world literature that he showed me. Given my circumstances, I could never dream of spending that much money all at once, but when he said I could split the payment up over ten months, I didn't need to hear any more of his awkward sales pitch. He left in a cheerful mood at having sold the books so easily, and started showing up every month after that, supposedly just to collect my next installment. Had he been only a book peddler, I would not have followed him out of Moon Hollow. But he, too, loved reading, and he kept me well-supplied in books. We fell in love with each other while reading the same books and talking and even arguing about them, just as Minwoo and I had once done. But his timid personality made it hard for him to make ends meet as a book peddler. I moved with him to his hometown of Incheon and started a new life with him, selling eggs and fruits and vegetables out of a small truck.*

And then she had a son. She wrote that she lived more or less happily for the next ten years without wanting for more. Her husband made up for his lack of sociability by being a hard worker, and he got them a small room with a jeonse lease, after which he started saving money bit by bit. The year their son turned ten, her husband was badly injured in a traffic accident and received no compensation.

As he lay bedridden, their debt mounted; by the time he died, she was back to square one. She took whatever work she could find, cleaning houses, helping out in restaurants, doing janitorial work. But the money she made was barely enough to cover the interest on their debt. She had no choice but to leave her young son at home alone while she worked. Fortunately, her son took after his father and grew up to be a polite boy who stayed out of trouble. He'd only graduated from a junior college since he didn't have the grades for university, and he was relegated to a temporary contract job, but at least it was at a major firm. Up until he was fired, he worked as an assistant on a demolition site; Soona described in detail how earnest and hard-working he was. I paused at the part where she said he worked on the wrecking crew of an area being redeveloped. The image was all too familiar, as if it were being reenacted right in front of me. My breath grew short, and I felt a strange tug, like there was some delicate, invisible string that connected us all to each other. She wrote that after her son was fired, he went from one part-time job to another before finally taking his own life last winter. When I looked up from her letter, barely an hour had gone by. All those decades of her tumultuous life had slipped into the past along with my hour of reading.

She said that she had spotted my name on a banner outside of City Hall while riding by on the bus one day. I turned back to the letter.

My heart raced when I saw your aged face in the photo. After my son died, I went back to Moon Hollow for the first time in a very long time. There was no trace left of our lives there. Your parents' fishcake shop, our noodle shop, the public tap, Jaemyung's shoeshine stand, the movie theatre, the overpass. It was all gone. Everything was so changed that I found myself wondering if that place had ever really existed. How could forty years fly by so quickly? So many waves of people coming and going in those streets, people who grew up there with us, people born after we left …

Ah, I almost forgot. I named my son Minwoo. Even though his childhood was as poor and difficult as ours, I wanted more than anything for him to be happy. Where did I go wrong? Why did my son's life have to end that way?

Her story ended there. For some reason I felt like she was scolding me. For a life story, it was quite short. Parts of my life story had been included, too. Each time I read one of her paragraphs, faces and images that had been frozen in time came back to me. I got up, feeling a mix of emotions, paced back and forth, and then stood in the window for a long time. I felt like my body was slowly disappearing. First my arms and legs blurred at the edges and vanished, leaving only my trunk, then that, too, started to disappear from the bottom up. I stared at the reflection of my upper half floating in the window, transposed over the city lights, like a photo taken from overlapping negatives. Who are you? asked the man in the glass.

Aren't you going to answer your phone?

My secretary was poking her head around the door. Just then I realised that my cell phone had been ringing away on my desk. As I reached for it, I asked the secretary,

Do we have any cigarettes?

She came back with a pack and some matches. I lit one and took a deep drag. I hadn't had a cigarette in so long that my head felt like it was spinning. I sat down hard in my chair. The person who'd called was Youngbin. I immediately asked where he was and what he was doing. He told me his second oldest was getting married and said he would send me an invitation. I suggested meeting for a drink. He sounded surprised and asked if something had happened. Today had been a mess, and tomorrow was still a question, so I said never mind, told him I'd call him up next time, and hung up. I smoked the cigarette slowly, the whole thing, until the filter started to burn. I gave in to the dizzy, sluggish feeling and sat there blankly for a long time.

I gazed at the computer screen for a moment, and then typed 'urban redevelopment' into a search engine. An endless list of links popped up; I scrolled through page after page of photos and text. By the time I'd returned to Korea with my wife and daughter after studying in the US, ten years had passed, and I was nearing forty. I'd acquired practical experience while working on several international projects in the US. That was when I joined Hyeonsan as a department head, right when business really took off for both the company and for me. I came across a photo of a residential redevelopment project that my old childhood friend Yoon Byeonggu and I had handled in the mid-1990s. Of course, that was around the same time that the Sampoong Department Store had collapsed. Nearly ninety per cent of the structures that had been built during modernisation failed to pass safety inspections, and even those that did pass were in need of repairs or renovation. But this did nothing to fix the irregularities and corruption that plagued construction at every stage, from planning to commencement to completion. Instead, it expanded the new market. That was when I started my own company, and Byeonggu went into politics. The photos online held the past and present of the urban redevelopment project that I'd participated in just ten years earlier.

I saw a mountain covered in low slate roofs, narrow winding alleys tangling around each other, smiling children clustered in front of a tiny shop. Where were they now, these people who found themselves pushed out of a neighbourhood they'd grown to love? Those little shacks clinging to the hillsides like barnacles had all vanished, and in their place mountainous concrete apartment buildings rose up and blocked out the sky. Half-collapsed houses and an abandoned car rusting on top of rubble sat at the edge of an empty field. Weeds that had sprung through cracks in the alleys where no one walked anymore formed a thicket, and in the corner of a devastated building, a scrawny stray dog loitered. Anti-demolition protesters, most of whom were women, held up picket signs scrawled in ungainly handwriting and shouted at the camera. I had witnessed all of this from a distance while out doing site inspections with Byeonggu. We always jumped back in the car and left in a hurry, right before the the demolition crews broke up the protesters and sent in the bulldozers and excavators, as if we couldn't bear to watch it ourselves.

Ah, and there. Finally, I saw the last image of the place where I'd grown up. That project had been headed up by another company, one that I knew well. My parents left Moon Hollow long before it was torn down and redeveloped, so I hadn't given a single thought to what had happened to it. If Soona had not contacted me, it would probably still be far from my mind. I saw the main road through the marketplace that I was all too used to, the familiar buildings and signs. In front of a shop, Myosoon and Soona were playing jacks, and Jaemyung, Jjaekkan, and I were playing a game where we hopped around on one leg and tried to knock each other down. The children in the photographs online were strangers, but they'd probably grown up in the same kind of place and dreamed the same kinds of dreams as we all did back then.

My memories were different from those of the

people who'd lived there. My job had been to shove their memories together into one big pile, sweep them away, and obliterate them. I knew all about the food chain that led from the guild that our consulting team had put together, to the design companies and demolition companies, to the construction companies and the district councils, all the way up to political circles. Byeonggu and I both knew how it worked, from all the countless meetings and rounds of drinks and games of golf, from all the meticulously detailed reports and receipts for gift certificates, designer goods, and hard cash. Byeonggu became a member of the National Assembly and got re-elected only to have to resign halfway through his term due to some unsavoury incident, but I helped him out several times. Actually, we had always needed each other. Byeonggu, the Burnt Sweet Potato who'd been reduced to a vegetable, now lay on a bed of memories that had vanished from Yeongsan, where he'd gotten his start. For a long time, I'd been thinking only that I was lucky enough to have escaped a squalid, shabby hillside slum. As if everyone who'd made it through that era were doing fine now. As if none of us had fallen through the cracks.

I checked my email inbox again and re-read the last line of Soona's letter.

Where did I go wrong? Why did my son's life have to end that way?

I clicked reply and wrote her a message.

Thank you for remembering an old friend. I should have written back to you much sooner. If you're okay with it, I would like to see you. Just let me know when and where. I look forward to hearing from you.

10

I put a kettle on for tea and sit at my desk to eat one of the triangle kimbap I brought with me from work. I'll eat the other two later, after I've slept. I turn on my laptop and look at the various folders on the desktop. One for downloaded movies, one for English conversation lessons, one for scripts that I've been working on, another for photos, and so on. The files I've been opening the most often lately are 'Foxtail' and 'Black Shirt'. As usual, the first things I look at online are the news headlines. One in particular catches my eye: the chairman of Daedong Construction arrested for embezzlement and malpractice. I skim the article and then check my email. One from my sister, another from my boss at the theatre proposing what our next project should be, and one from Mr Park. Now that he has suggested meeting in person, the time has finally come for me to bring this game to an end.

After Minwoo died, I spent every weekend in Bucheon with his mother. I guess you could say we depended on each other. Minwoo's absence had me feeling more and more out of control as time passed. I blamed myself for being so indifferent towards him, as if his death were my fault. But after a while, it was like what Minwoo's mother said: the living have to go on living. She and I ate together, drank together, and even laughed together. As my friends would say, she was a cool mum. She was literally old enough to be my mum, but she felt more like a close friend. Maybe, too, it was a certain pureness that came from her having been so immersed in literature as a teenager, or even a childlike naivety, but whatever it was, something about her made it easy for us to relate to each other.

One day, when the season of Minwoo's death had passed and the spring blossoms were in full bloom, she and I went downtown to have a beer. There, she told me about how she'd been raped as a teenager. She remembered every detail, but told it like it was nothing. That was when I realised that she'd been keeping a notebook. She asked me to show her how to use a computer, and started transferring her handwritten notes to the laptop Minwoo had left behind. She proudly told me that graduating from an all-girls high school and working as a bookkeeper, where she'd learned to type, had come in handy. I asked her what she was writing.

I guess you could call it my memoirs. A kind of reminder to myself that I've been through a lot but I lived a good life, she said.

I immediately understood what she meant. Journalling or writing letters to someone when you're struggling or having a hard time can sometimes cause you to wallow even more, but it is also very healing.

Then one day, the moment she saw me, she told me excitedly that a close childhood friend of hers was giving a lecture at City Hall. She told me about growing up in the hillside slum, and rattled off the whole story of their friendship. Halfway through, I got impatient and interrupted her.

This man you're talking about has the same name as Minwoo. Is he ... Minwoo's father?

She laughed and teased me about trying to turn it into a soap opera.

Let's go to the lecture together, I said. I bet he'll be happy to see you.

She shook her head. I'm so chubby now. He'll be disappointed. She looked down at herself and let out a sigh. He left Moon Hollow and me behind a long time ago. He lives in another world now.

I went to the lecture without telling her. I waited for the lecture to end, and I handed him a note with her name and phone number. When I told her later what I'd done, she frowned and scolded me.

Where did you get such a stupid idea? she said.

I suggested that we place bets, hoping to trick her out of staying angry at me.

Don't be ridiculous. Even if he does call, I'll just say it's the wrong number.

Still, I bet you 50,000 won he'll call.

100,000 won says he won't!

So if he does call, you'll give me 100,000 won? For real?

Late one night, when I'd nearly forgotten all about the bet, she called me. She sounded drunk. She said that Park Minwoo had called her but she didn't answer, and now there was a text message from him. She wasn't an alcoholic, but ever since Minwoo had died, she'd been drinking more and more. I warned her that she shouldn't drink alone, what with her blood pressure, but she told me in a slurred voice that alcohol made the hours pass faster. Makes day and night fly right by, she said. I started to fuss at her again, but she cut me off in a flat voice.

The greatest blessing is to die in your sleep, so why not.

I decided to visit her that weekend and jokingly demand that she pay me 100,000 won. But the part-time worker who normally worked the weekend shift at the convenience store quit suddenly, and I had to fill in for him. The next weekend, I was overwhelmed with theatre rehearsals and opening night preparations. I didn't even have time to talk on the phone, so we just texted back and forth. One day she texted that she'd finally talked to the architect. I pushed her to meet him in person, but she adamantly refused.

Then, that morning, when I had finished up at the

convenience store and was on my way home, I got her last
text message.

> Heading home? Bet you're exhausted. You said
> opening night is tomorrow, right? If I can't make
> it then, I'll go the next day. It's been a while.
> Miss you.

But she didn't come that week or the next week.

I've kept in my room some of the things she left behind.
She died in her sleep, the blessed passing that she'd joked
about, and only a few months after her son had passed, as
if she were rushing to catch up to him. She died of a stroke
while wrapped up in her blankets at home.

I was the one who found her. The play was in its third
week and was only one more week from finishing, but she
wasn't the type to just not show and not even call. I tried
contacting her but got no responses to my texts, and each
time I dialled her number, her cell was turned off. I had
a feeling something was wrong, so I went straight to her
place after my shift at the convenience store. The door
to her apartment was plastered with fliers and delivery
menus for Chinese food and other places nearby. I rang
the doorbell. No response. I rang it several more times, but
all I heard was the chiming of the doorbell echoing inside
her apartment. I knew the code to the digital lock. It was
Kim Minwoo's birthdate.

The second I opened the door, I smelled something terrible. When I turned on the light, the first thing I saw was a low folding table in the middle of the living room covered in soju and beer bottles. I opened her bedroom door and saw a gray leathery face peeking out over the soiled hem of her blanket. I covered my mouth and hesitated a moment, then ran to find the building superintendent. The police came, and the next day a simple autopsy was performed. Her funeral was as quick and businesslike as Minwoo's. I guess having one less person in the world didn't cause much of a stir. People die everyday for all kinds of reasons, and new ones are born. Death and life are just ordinary occurrences.

The police asked if I was an immediate relative. I insisted that I was her son's fiancee. That's how I was able to hold onto Minwoo's laptop and the cardboard boxes stuffed with photo albums and the five thick spiral-bound notebooks that she'd been writing in. Once I had the photo albums in my room though, I realised I shouldn't have bothered with those. I didn't know what to do with all the photos. I decided to hold onto them for the time being, and to later take them to the quiet riverside in Chungju where Minwoo had died, and burn them there.

As I was carrying the last of her items out of the apartment, I noticed a flowerpot in the corridor outside her front door. It was overgrown with foxtails. They were yellowed and starting to wither, as if they'd been neglected for a while. I told myself she couldn't possibly have planted them on purpose, that the seeds must have been blown into the pot by the wind and sprouted there. But at the same time, someone must have watered them for them to grow that lush in the first place.

*

Lately, I've been absorbed in reading her memoirs. She wrote so much. I don't know when she had time to do all that typing; she'd already transferred the contents of one of her big notebooks to the laptop. The originals were fairly rough, but it looked like she'd edited them as she typed. With a little more editing, it would be publishable. Then one day, while reading, I had a crazy idea. I knew who her first reader should be.

I started using my spare time to create an abridged version of her journals, just like writing a treatment, and contacted him using her name. I already knew a lot about him. Several times a day I looked up news articles and information on him online. Each time I wrote to him, I became Cha Soona of Moon Hollow. I even had a dream one night where I took his hand and walked out of this basement room. I dreamt that I'd come back from the convenience store and had fallen asleep in the middle of writing. A heavy rain poured down, and muddy water surged down the stairs into my room. In a flash, the room was submerged. As I floundered, Kim Minwoo reached out to me and said we had to go now. I grabbed his hand and barely made it out. But when I looked, it was the other Minwoo, Mr Park.

It's time now for me to exit the stage. I reply to Mr Park's email. Jung Woohee and Cha Soona clamour and compete for the spotlight. But as soon as my fingers touch the keyboard, I become her. Dear Minwoo, I would love to see you, too …

I arrive at the location an hour early to take a look around. I don't know what it looked like back then, but it doesn't have any of the charm that I'd seen in Minwoo's mother's writing. The ridgeline bristles with apartment buildings; the whole place looks like a fortress. Clusters of leaves turning colour cling to tall trees that are just starting to bare their branches. Pines and firs line the paved roads. A young mother pushes a stroller down a sidewalk blanketed in red, orange, and yellow leaves. Children play with a white puppy. Their clear peals of laughter rise into the air.

I walk downhill from the apartment buildings to a hotel on the main street. I heard that it used to be a movie theatre. I go to the lounge on the top floor and sit in the very back, next to the window. I had scouted out the location already and decided where I would sit. The floor-to-ceiling windows face east; the afternoon shadows are advancing. The apartment buildings block all view of the mountains.

At the agreed-upon time, Mr Park enters. He wears a dark gray suit with no tie. When he glances around, I lower my head to avoid his eyes. He comes over to the window and stands there a moment, looking out. Maybe he's looking for some trace of the old neighbourhood. A waiter comes and leads him to a table. He takes his time sitting down, facing away from me. Right in front of me is his gray hair and the bald spot at the top of his head. His shoulders are slumped, causing the back of his jacket to bunch up. Elderly men always look a little melancholy from behind. He keeps gazing out the window, then swiveling his head toward the entrance, as if suddenly remembering something. He is facing his past, but his past is my present. He pushes up his sleeve to check his watch. Twenty minutes have passed already. I get up and walk over to him. When I am right next to him, his phone rings. He answers it.

Yes, it's Dad. How are you?

I keep walking quietly past and go outside. I don't know how long he'll stay there, but I don't think it will take long for him to realise that there is no point in waiting. I might have to be Cha Soona for a while longer. It makes my life bearable, and there's still more story to be told. Some of it is my story, and some of it is Cha Soona's unfinished story.

• • •

My daughter told me that she was coming to Korea for the winter. Her husband was on sabbatical and wanted to come, too. I accidentally blurted out, And your mother? Just us, she said. She was quiet for a moment, and then said, Really, Dad, how come you've never visited even once? She sounded resentful.

I waited thirty more minutes after hanging up, but Soona didn't come. I debated whether to wait a little longer, but then thought better of it and got up to leave. She was the one who picked this place, so why didn't she show up?

Outside, the sun was already setting. Beneath the trees heavy with autumn foliage, yellowed foxtails were waving in the breeze.

Look at this. The housekeeper says it's all weeds. You can tell them apart by their colour. They're lighter than grass. Grass grows together neatly, but with these, you have to rake around them one by one with a hoe and yank them out by the roots.

My wife used to love explaining this sort of thing to me at great length, as if it were some amazing fact, all while pulling weeds from the yard and showing them to me. I would sit on the deck under a sun umbrella and glance over at her to pretend I was listening, then turn back to the newspaper.

They grow so fast that if you don't do anything about them, they'll destroy your lawn. See? How they're spread all over the lawn?

Every summer, my wife liked to sit in the yard and grumble and pull weeds. After returning from the US and going into architecture, nearly a decade passed before I got around to buying land in a new suburb of Seoul and building a house of my own design. Initially, my wife hated the idea of pulling weeds and getting her hands dirty, but the other women in the neighbourhood got together every spring and went around in twos and threes to plant flowers. Seeing that triggered my wife's competitive side. She was a neat freak who liked to keep up with the neighbours and couldn't stand anything unsightly. She became temporarily obsessed with fixing up the yard, and planted the garden with all sort of rare wildflowers. The yard was tiny, but it took a lot of work to cultivate it. Once the house was built, I claimed that I was too busy to do anything else, and besides, I had no interest in doing yardwork. My wife asked why I'd insisted on moving into a house with a yard if I was going to be that way, and complained endlessly about how scary it was to be alone in the house at night.

I found myself wondering when we'd started planting grass in yards anyway. Traditionally, courtyards were lined with sand or dirt, with a small flowerbed near the wall planted with rose moss, balsam, asters, hydrangea, or with vegetables. Grass didn't even make sense in our climate, and besides, the only place we really planted grass in Korea was on top of graves. And yet, from some point on, grass started showing up in people's yards and came to signify that they were middle-class. One day, I was standing out in the yard and debating whether to just plow up all the grass and replace it with sand when I spotted some familiar, downy-looking plants poking up among the flowers. My wife and the housekeeper had missed a few while weeding, and now they'd revealed their identity. It was foxtails. I walked over to pull them from the earth, but stopped myself. They looked kind of nice there, mixed in with the flowers that had been planted on purpose.

My wife and I did not live in that house for long. In the end, I gave in to my wife's nagging and moved us to an 'officetel' — an apartment in a high-rise, mixed-use building that was all the rage in Gangnam at the time. Our marriage gradually worsened beyond the point of recovery. As my wife started spending more and more time with our daughter, I decided to move to a townhouse instead. Those high-rise officetels never did sit right with me. I'm not crazy about this current house either. Nowadays, my only pleasure is poring over online maps for new plots of land and imagining the kind of house I would build. But I have no family to live in that house with me.

And so there I stood, in the middle of the sidewalk in what was once Moon Hollow, like a man who'd lost his way.